Girl from the Racetrack

St Michael the Archangel, defend us in Battle...
Cathedral of Notre Dame
SAIGON, VIETNAM – 1972

Girl

From the
Racetrack

A Novel of the Vietnam War

Robert Brundrett

Orange *frazer* Press
Wilmington, Ohio

ISBN 978-1949248-500
Copyright ©2021 Robert L. Brundrett
All Rights Reserved

No part of this publication may be reproduced in any material form (including photocopying or storing in any medium by electronic means and whether or not transiently or incidentally to some other use of this publication) without the written permission of the copyright holder except in accordance with the provisions of Title 17 of the United States Code.

Published for the copyright holder by:
Orange Frazer Press
37½ West Main St.
P.O. Box 214
Wilmington, OH 45177

For price and shipping information, call: 937.382.3196
Or visit: www.orangefrazer.com

Book and cover design by:
Orange Frazer Press with Catie South

Back cover image by Jongsun Lee. Imported from 500px (archived version) by the Archive Team. (detail page), CC BY 3.0, https://commons.wikimedia.org/w/index.php?curid=71587893

Library of Congress Control Number: 2021916633

This is a work of fiction. Names, characters, incidents, places and events are either the product of the author's imagination or used fictionally. Any resemblance to actual persons, living or dead, businesses, companies, events or locals is entirely coincidental.

First Printing

This book is dedicated in memory of

James C. Brundrett
(1947 – 2020)

First Lieutenant, 23rd Infantry,
AMERICAL Division
Vietnam, 1971

"It is not the critic who counts; not the man who points out how the strong man stumbles, or where the doer of deeds could have done them better. The credit belongs to the man who is actually in the arena … "

—Theodore Roosevelt, April, 1910

Acknowledgment

I would like to acknowledge the help and inspiration given to me by my wife, Linda, for the creation of this book. The time she took to review chapters, her solid advice and her confidence in me to complete this book were so important in making it happen.

Table of Contents

Prologue	xiii
Part One	1
Part Two	209
Epilogue	231

Prologue

Charlie Strickland was my roommate at Ohio State. We lived together in Stradley Hall for four years during the 1960s. It was the time of The Vietnam War. A couple of years after college Charlie found himself, as many of us did, inevitably heading to Vietnam. And so, after OCS (Officer Candidate School) and some Asian culture training, the day came in January, 1972, when he boarded an airplane and flew all night to Southeast Asia. It was 6 a.m. the next morning when the plane landed to refuel and take a quick breakfast break at Clark Air Force Base (AFB) in the Philippines before flying the short hop on to South Vietnam. Charlie stepped off the aircraft into a warm and muggy semi-dark dawn. He breathed in the thick air filled with strange smells and stretched his cramped legs. He was greeted by smiling Filipina ladies who served the American service men donuts and coffee. By 8 a.m., the aircraft was back in the air and streaking across the Pacific sky to Vietnam.

Charlie's young life had been full of many experiences, but somehow the new day brought with it something very different. With the early morning sun at his back, he watched from the aircraft the strange tropical land unfolding below him. As the DC-8 rushed in at low altitude to Saigon, Charlie felt an inexplicable surge of excitement that foretold he would henceforth measure time as before or after Vietnam.

Charlie once told me his first impressions of Vietnam were the 100-degree day, the sweet smells of Asia, and a barefoot kid slow-trotting a nice looking thoroughbred colt down Plantation Road. Of all the things Charlie expected to find when he landed in Vietnam, horse racing was certainly not one of them. But find it he did: thoroughbred-style horse racing in the middle of the war. The sport of kings and the lust for gambling would not be denied because of the occasional afternoon mortar attack on Saigon.

The racing occurred at the large Phu Tho track built by the French in 1932 along Plantation Road, the main artery between Saigon proper and Tan Son Nhut Airbase. Nearly all horses came from local farms in the Mekong River Delta, in the vicinity of Saigon. Most were brought in on race day. In some cases they were stabled overnight in rented sheds near Plantation Road. It was not uncommon to see racehorses being led by grooms through heavy traffic on streets near Plantation Road.

Charlie liked horses. He had grown up with them on his family's farm in Ohio. He was now a lieutenant with the Navy engineers assigned to help the Vietnamese Navy with boat design and architecture. He was naturally delighted to discover horse racing and hoped for the opportunity to experience it sometime while "in-country." As it turned out, he found much more than horse racing.

Prologue

My name is Joe, Joe Savage. I'm not a big war hero or anything. I'm just the narrator. Oh, I may show up in the story a few times, but this story is really about two people: Charlie and Kim. It was in Vietnam that Charlie met Kim. I was there with Charlie for most of his time in Vietnam, so I'm rather well positioned to tell this story and I decided it was one that should be told. It's the type of story that didn't make the evening news. It was squeezed out by headlines of horrific bombing and killing that's become the sad legacy of the only war they say we ever lost. It's the love story of a boy and a girl. What they thought, what they did, and what they risked for each other. It's just one story in the broad spectrum of altered lives because of Vietnam.

Part One

Chapter One

The Racetrack

This story starts on a sun-filled afternoon in Saigon in February, 1972. Charlie had been "in-country" for only a month. The war was in its eleventh year. A man stood against a chain-link fence that separated the one-and-a-quarter-mile Phu Tho Racetrack from its ornate old viewing stands and watched the horses line up in the starting gate. The third race of the afternoon was up. The man's name was Nguyen Binh Li, a middle-aged Vietnamese gentleman who was retired from the military with a medical discharge and now a horse trainer.

Most people knew him as Binh. He was ordinary in appearance, except for a distinctively kind face lined by years of hard work and terrifying war experiences. Square shoulders of hard farmer muscle gave evidence of physical stamina. His calloused hands clung to the rusted wire fence as he strained older yet alert eyes to see the girl on the gray colt that carried Number 6. Binh wore a sportsman's hat, a white short-sleeved shirt and faded working class black serge trousers. Laced up above his ankles were a pair of well-worn French Legionnaire combat boots he'd acquired from a good friend years ago when his battalion returned to France.

Binh always stood just outside the fence and perhaps fifty meters up the track when he had a horse in the race: a good place to view the horses face-on as they broke from the starting gate. Binh watched very closely this day. It was his daughter that sat atop Number 6.

He looked around. Close by Binh at the rear of the stands were a few old women sitting on their heels and chattering. They were cooking their midday meal squatting on the ground with their cooking pans and gas heaters. A few pedicab drivers sat on their three-wheeled cycles and waited for fares from the track while smoking cheap dark cigarettes. The stands were filled with local Vietnamese or Chinese men. There were also a few French men and women—and occasionally British men of the older generation—in their summer-weight suits.

This region of Plantation Road in those days was generally an unsavory place, and one would not normally want to linger here. The afternoon sun was hot and the air was thick. Heavy traffic moved slowly along, noisy with scooters, buses, jeeps and Blue and White Renault taxis travelling to and from the airport. Plantation Road was paved but seemed more like a dirt and gravel road due to continual dust generated by the heavy diesel military vehicles. Prostitutes hung out on street corners where shade existed. They sometimes could be heard laughing and flirting with waving GIs. They often got their point across with obscene gestures and profanity as they smiled at their unending source of revenue.

Two streets back and parallel to Plantation Road lay a sad shanty town of hundreds, perhaps thousands, of tiny houses. They were constructed of cardboard and corrugated sheet metal often attached to and supporting one another. It was a community of tightly packed humanity built up by thousands of refugees who migrated there to escape the war in the countryside. There were also a number of young AWOL GIs suffering from battle fatigue or trauma, drug or alcohol addiction, or those hopelessly lost in the entropy of war. It was the era of "tuning in and dropping out," and the war did nothing to improve that state of mind. Many small streams and tributaries of the Saigon River wandered through this area. The streams were nearly black in color and emitted an unwelcome odor, a metaphor for the poor contaminated lives in this hellish sub-culture.

It was not the nice side of town, but once one passed onto the race grounds property the atmosphere changed. The viewing stands and track still held some of the mystique of colonial times and the artistic flair of French pride that existed in the century-old architecture. There were still the old palm trees that framed the flowered entrance. The entrance facade was now no doubt financially supported by the older generation French desperate to hold on to their "Pearl of the Orient."

A Blue and White taxi pulled up to the racetrack and a US Navy man named Charlie Strickland emerged from the small Renault. With Charlie was his Vietnamese counterpart, Lieutenant Dao. Although from different parts of the world, the American with the athletic six-foot frame and the Vietnamese man of slight stature had much in common. Both were graduate engineers, analytical thinkers, and driven by stubborn optimism.

Dao reached back into the car and handed the driver a five hundred-piaster note. The two Navy officers walked into the viewing area, passing by the old women and Binh as they reached seats in the first row. They sat back to review the racing card, and that's when all the trouble started.

Chapter One

An angry whip crack and a profane oath shouted at a horse split the thick afternoon air. An abrupt clang was heard as a horse slammed into the starting gate. It was horse Number 6. Something had spooked the animal and suddenly a situation had developed. Track workers quickly latched the rear stanchion gate so the frightened animal could not back out. The horse began rearing and challenging the bounds of the starting stanchion. The girl jockey was trying desperately to maintain control of her horse, but the terrified animal kept rearing and striking out at the forward gate. All eyes were on Number 6 and an audible murmur floated across the crowd with each collision. Binh furrowed his brow as the gray horse screamed. The starting bell rang out and the horses launched.

Propelled by terror, the gray ran wildly across the track in front of Binh while the girl attempted to control it. Horses collided but continued and the girl somehow stayed on the horse. With extreme effort she seemed to regain control, but the horse had been hurt and seconds later crashed into another horse. The girl was thrown from the animal as the horse went down with unknown injuries, unable to rise. The horse trailing Number 6 leaped over the fallen jockey, stumbled, and continued. Two other horses were hurt in the melee and unable to continue. With three horses injured and a jockey lying unconscious on the track, the race was stopped and the emergency crew dispatched to the site.

Charlie had jumped up to better see the action; he was so close to the downed and struggling animal that he couldn't resist running to its aid. He found the horse's leg tangled in the breast harness. He skillfully freed the animal, taking care to keep clear of a wildly kicking rear leg. The horse rose to its feet slowly and stood still, breathing hard, with its head down and favoring his left front hoof. Charlie advised the track emergency attendant that he suspected a cracked or severely strained pastern on the left front that needed immediate attention. Then Charlie saw the jockey.

Binh had already gone to the aid of his daughter. The jockey lay with face turned away about ten meters back down the track from the horse. Binh had climbed the fence and arrived just as Charlie did.

"Best not move him!" he cried to Binh. "You could damage his neck." Binh paid no attention and was already removing his daughter's helmet. Long black hair spilled out and Charlie cried, "Well, I'll be damned!" She was unconscious and unmoving; Binh studied her earnestly and began to unsnap her tight silk neck collar, talking to her in a comforting manner. Suddenly, her eyes opened and she looked up at the two men.

"My daughter," Binh said as he managed a relieved smile. The girl looked at Charlie and said, "American," then fell back unconscious.

Chapter Two

The 1960s

Charlie and I had parted ways after college. He stayed at school and began an internship with one of the professors he admired. I think he always had in mind to teach math and engineering. But this was about the time that the lottery for the draft began. Both of our fathers had served in WWII. We were true baby boomers and both the ripe age for the draft.

It was the 1960s, a time of turmoil in America, especially for young men and women. So many changes were taking place it was difficult to keep up with them. Charlie and I went to Ohio State in 1963 as the last embers of the 1950s culture were dying, and came out in 1968 to a changed America and world.

I was walking across the Oval to chemistry class on November 22, 1963, when President Kennedy was shot. That seemed to hasten an era of unrest that included an explosion of Civil Rights issues, race riots in large cities, assassinations, LSD, hippies, free love, protest marches against the War, the burning of draft cards, a large generational gap between young and old on opinions of the War, and a general mistrust of the government.

The Vietnam War was the big sore in American society that would not heal. It was in everyone's face, every day. Hundreds of young Americans were killed each week. The first war that was broadcast in real time, unfiltered and seen nightly on TV news. All in living color. And it went on year after year. Charlie and I both had doubts about the war. But busy with technical courses, we didn't take time to think about it much in college; we trusted Uncle Sam to do what was right for America.

As the '60s generation went on with their lives, decisions were made. Some were overtaken by events without making decisions. Of those who ended up in Vietnam, many found their lives forever altered. And the lives of individuals and families attached to the veterans were changed as well. But it was only after I got to Vietnam that I realized the Vietnamese people could say the same, except to a much larger degree. They lived the terror of war night and day. And yet their lives went on.

Charlie had a low draft number, so instead of being drafted he signed up for Navy OCS. As for myself, I took a job with a defense contractor but didn't like it, got bored, and also joined the Navy. Amazingly, we found ourselves in Vietnam as Navy engineers—at the same time and same place. Actually, I arrived there about two months before Charlie and through a special arrangement due to family issues had signed up for sixteen months. Charlie's obligation was the normal twelve months in-country hitch. I was with the Construction Bureau and travelled throughout the Mekong River Delta on building projects with my Vietnamese counterpart, Lieutenant Danh. I lived in downtown Saigon on Hai Ba Trung Street (Two Sisters Street) in a BOQ (Bachelor Officer Quarters) for Navy engineers. Charlie worked with the boat designers and lived at a BOQ right in the Saigon shipyard where he worked with the Vietnamese trying to introduce badly needed newer technology to their designs.

I first realized Charlie was in Vietnam when Lieutenant Danh and I went to inspect a high-powered pump we needed for a water treatment plant and found the engineers were trying to fit the same pump into a Navy "skimmer" speed boat. Two men in Navy fatigues were under the boat on their backs sweating like pigs trying to connect the propulsion jets. One of them was swearing like a drunken sailor. I could hardly believe it when I heard that voice, because I recognized it instantly. "I haven't heard that kind of cussing since my roommate was cramming for a math final!" I shouted down at him.

Charlie looked up at me and shouted back, "Didn't help me then and still doesn't."

We both started howling and couldn't stop. That was January of '72, and afterward we saw each other nearly every day.

Chapter Three

Kim

The girl at the racetrack was Nguyen Kim Li. Her friends called her Kim. She was nineteen when Charlie met her. She had already finished high school, having attended one of the better Catholic schools in Saigon. Her education was partially funded by the State because her father was a war veteran, and because Catholic education had been a priority for the assassinated President Diem, a Catholic himself. The family had moved from heavily Catholic North Vietnam during the 1955 migration from North to South, assisted by the US Navy.

Kim had been recognized for top marks in school, but was thus far prevented from pursuing a career in art due to the confusion of war. Filling in as a jockey when necessary and helping to train the horses with her trainer father provided some funds for potential art studies. But Kim also loved horses and had the physical ability and manner to handle them with good results. She was known around the track as an expert horsewoman, and would often be given troublesome horses.

She was striking in appearance, slender but not frail, with the essence of gold in her skin found in traditional poetry and music of Vietnam. Her face was a perfect oval of delicate features. Like most young Vietnamese women, Kim wore her flowing obsidian hair long and straight. She had an open manner among others, flowing easily in and out of conversations and languages.

She was a presence in a room, not only for her appearance but her poise and confidence. Kim was not without suitors but seemed always able to navigate her own life as she desired. She would never let herself be steered by others, but always appeared friendly and gentle. Others often looked to her for a calming influence. Because of this she presented older and wiser than nineteen. When Charlie first introduced me to Kim, I knew he was in trouble.

Chapter Four

Captain Eagleton

Charlie knocked on Captain Eagleton's open office door. Eagleton sat at his massive desk but did not look up. It was a trait of Eagleton's to require one to wait for an audience at the captain's pleasure. An additive reason, of course, was to make sure it appeared he was busy with important captain business at hand.

Captain Eagleton was in charge of the US Navy Technical Group at the VN Navy shipyard. He also had the responsibility of senior advisor at the shipyard. In this role, he was Charlie's and my immediate supervisor. The captain was not a young man, and he was not going to make it to admiral. This was probably his twilight tour, or if not, certainly next to twilight. He was old school Navy: stern manner, immaculate uniform, closely cropped hair. He was of average height in stature but getting quite thick around the middle, which had the effect of making him look shorter than his actual

Chapter Four

height. His barrel chest, however, gave ample room for a full display of ribbons and awards.

The captain could never be mistaken for a friendly man. I'm not sure if he'd been this way throughout his career, or if it was just Vietnam. His facial expression seemed set, no matter his mood, and could only be described by the word "disdain." A disdain for his surroundings, and disdain for the native people in his surroundings. He wore his racist views on his sleeve. Selecting Captain Eagleton for his probable twilight role of working closely with foreign nationals certainly seemed off the mark.

He was cast in a job that primarily required him to "advise and teach," whereas he knew only how to "command." He thought little of his real job of managing and advising the Vietnamese engineers and architects on research and development of their facilities and small Navy ships.

Charlie waited patiently until Eagleton finally looked up and acknowledged him.

"You asked to see me, sir."

"Yes, come in, Strickland."

Charlie was a tall six feet, and the captain did not like to be looking up at anyone.

"Please sit down, Strickland."

"Thank you, sir."

Looking over things on his desk, he began: "How are things going, Lieutenant; you've been here for over a month now? Things going well, are they? That is, except of course for that messy business with those horse people at the racetrack."

He looked at Charlie and asked, "I assume all that business is behind us now?"

"Oh, yes, sir, I played only a small part in that incident. It was interesting to become acquainted with the surrounding area and the local people, though, and to experience it with my counterpart, Lieutenant Dao. He's a smart engineer and good teacher. I'm hoping to gain his trust so we can work together in developing some of the new technology for their Navy. We'll have a new version of the VNN high speed skimmer speed-boat ready for trial in a couple of weeks."

"Okay, that's fine," the Captain said, "but a word to the wise: don't get too close to these people. You can never completely trust them, you know. Remember, they aren't like us; they have their own religions and habits and so forth."

"Oh, I think the people that Dao and I met at the racetrack seem pretty normal. They are actually Catholic, like myself. In fact, Dao is Catholic also."

Then in a rather stern way that surprised Charlie, the Captain said, "Lieutenant, believe me, I've been around this world a long time, and I'm telling you these people are nothing like you and I. They are backward and somewhat feeble-minded. Their hygiene standards are what one would expect in a Third World country. Just a word to the wise. You understand, of course?"

"Yes, sir, captain."

"That will be all, Lieutenant Strickland."

Charlie went away scratching his head and wondering where the Captain was coming from. His Advisor Training in California less than six weeks before had emphasized the opposite of the Captain's words. Charlie was to learn that this was only the first of several times their opinions would differ.

Chapter Five

The Horse Farm

Charlie and Dao took Highway 13 and motored about ten miles south of Saigon toward Nha Be, then turned off on a small provincial road. They were on a mission: Charlie had received a note from the trainer at the racetrack, Binh, inviting him to their small farm. It seemed a gesture of gratitude for his help with the gray horse. Charlie had decided to ignore the captain's "word to the wise" and go ahead with the day trip.

I learned of this the prior evening at a waterfront bar where Charlie stood me to a 33 Export, his new favorite beer, which was brewed in Vietnam. "Don't understand where he got my name or how to get in touch," he said.

"Beats me, but it sounds legit," I told him. The harbor lights gleamed across the slow moving Saigon River as we talked. "It's like I said, they always know more than we do." Charlie was acting like he didn't know if he should go or not. "Charlie, my man, you know you're going and, besides, it's your duty to mingle with the locals, you being an advisor and all!" I goaded him. Even back then, Charlie was clearly more curious about the girl than the horse. "But make sure you take Dao with you. No Lone Ranger stuff. It's not *that* safe down there."

Charlie's Vietnamese counterpart, Dao, was equal rank to Charlie, a lieutenant in the Vietnamese Navy (VNN) and like Charlie he enjoyed math and technical stuff. He was married and had two young kids. He had a friendly smile and a hank of shaggy black hair. Dao was smart and a mild mannered "Joe Schmoe" regular guy. He was the kind of guy who liked to sit down with a cold beer and a Rubik's Cube. He paid his taxes, and if he lived in the US would probably have been a member of a Moose Lodge. He was savvy in the field, though, and a good shot. This morning he had come by with the Navy Ford Bronco, after he dropped the kids off at school.

The Bronco was not as rugged as the Jeep but it rode better, as long as you stayed on decent roads. Charlie and Dao studied the map and saw the horse farm was within five miles of the town of Nha Be. Dao needed some engine parts in Nha Be, so the plan was to drop Charlie off at the farm and Dao would pick him up on the way back. They'd gassed up at the shipyard and took off on their little trip.

To say Charlie was naïve in his perceptions of the social groups in the Mekong Delta would have been an understatement. The Army of the Republic of Vietnam (ARVN), usually kept the peace during the day, but the Viet Minh (the Communist insurgency in South Vietnam, often referred to as Viet Cong) owned the night. Sympathizers on both sides were operating there. As for religions, it was a split of Catholics, Buddhists, and Taoists, among others, each with their own ways of dealing with the warring factions. And a recent crackdown by

Chapter Five

the government on Buddhists speaking out against the ruling party had left the countryside with an uneasiness between neighbors.

I'll also say, however, that Charlie was an open-minded guy. Raised on a farm in central Ohio by a worldly mother (a US citizen who'd lived in France during WWII) and a kind old farmer father, he was about as unbiased and broad-minded as it comes. Because of his nature, Charlie made it his business to learn the ways of the people and the lay of the land. For this, he took full advantage of Dao's knowledge. By the time his tour was up, he was more savvy than most.

They drove down the provincial road slowly for it was barely more than a surface of hard-packed red clay. They passed a few pedestrians and two boys on bicycles. They proceeded on and crossed a low bridge just six feet above water level. Charlie looked down the water line and could see it was a narrow canal. A few small fishing sampans and boats carrying what appeared to be goods-to-market. The small vessels travelled slowly, propelled by single small gasoline engines. They were steered by long propeller shafts that entered the water at a shallow angle just below the water level. Their engines made a quiet put-putting noise while rippling the water as they passed under the bridge. After another half-mile of travel, just past one of the surviving Colonial French stone watch towers, Charlie recognized the road signs that Binh had described and pulled the Bronco over. He parked under some heavily leaved trees and brush.

They climbed out of the vehicle. It was a sunny day: lazy, hazy, and humid. Dao lit a cigarette, drew a big drag, and scanned the area with an alert eye. So thick and luscious were the large leaves and fauna that the vehicle was nearly hidden. After some searching, Charlie spotted the nearly hidden entrance to Binh's lane and told Dao he'd take it from there.

"Will two hours give you enough time in Nha Be?"

"Plenty." Then: "You're sure about this? You're kind of in the boonies here, Charlie."

"Don't worry, this is the place. I can smell horses, I'll be alright; see you in two hours, then."

Dao reached into the Bronco and handed Charlie his Navy Colt pistol and said, "At least carry this; I wouldn't walk down there unarmed myself."

"Thanks, Dao, be safe."

Dao backed the Ford out of the brush and was off. Charlie buckled on the Colt and looked at the entrance. There was a small sign that read: *Trai Ngua Da Mat Troi*, which translates, *Sun Stone Horse Farm*. The sign led to a pathway wrapped in a palate of greens and browns, with a sprinkle of color from wild flowers. It was dense and high climbing so that it provided shade and coolness with a multitude of tiny light beams streaming through.

The path brought memories of his family's farm and the lane to the back fields he would walk as a child: two tracks in the dirt worn by tractors, hay wagons, and farm equipment. Fence rows on both sides were full of wild growth of multi-floral rose, poison ivy brush, raspberry brambles, and tall weeds. The Holstein herd walked the lane daily in single file out to the rear pastures after morning milking and back in for the evening one. He could remember the summer heat and the sounds of buzzing insects and the distinct call of red-winged black birds in the adjacent hayfields. He chuckled as he found himself searching the high grass for a timothy stem to chew on.

Charlie walked down the path a bit farther. Soon the path broke out into an open area and Charlie realized he was walking on a paddy dike. Off to his left was a flooded paddy field. Beyond the paddy

Chapter Five

was another dike along a narrow canal. *Perhaps the same canal we just crossed,* he thought.

The unmistakable smell of horses became stronger and made him feel secure. The tree line continued on the right side of the path, then became sparse and finally disappeared as he continued. On his right, Charlie could see horse fencing surrounding a few acres of pasture. Beyond the pasture he could see an exercise track. Charlie stopped to take it all in when he became aware of Binh approaching in the distance. Binh was soon before him and, with an earnest smile, he offered a friendly farmer's hand. Charlie grasped it and the two shook vigorously.

"Welcome to my farm. I'm Binh … you're Lieutenant Strickland!"

"Yes, we meet."

Binh was wearing the same type of work clothes that he wore at the track, right down to the tough old leather boots. The only difference in dress was a Vietnamese conical hat in place of the sportsman's "track" hat.

From under his wide hat Nguyen looked directly at Charlie with clear eyes and a darkly tanned and lined face that surrounded an honest smile and said, "I'm happy you came!" Charlie liked him immediately. "It's our family farm. My family is waiting to greet you," he said as he gestured toward his house.

"And your daughter, is she well now?"

"Yes, quite well. Perhaps you speak French?"

"No, sorry, I don't, only English but wish I did right now. Why do you ask?"

"Oh, you remind me of someone," Binh smiled. "You know, many Vietnamese speak French. It's a little easier than English for us. I speak English okay but not perfect."

They both chuckled. Charlie noticed Binh walked with a slight limp as they continued on. They approached a small family vegetable and flower garden in front of a very neat one-story house. The house was surrounded by large leaved fauna tucked between breadfruit and coconut palm trees. It looked more modern than Charlie would have expected. A framed front door stood behind a tiled rectangular shaped front patio. At the four corners were red clay pots that held small bonsai plants reaching toward a light overhead structure from which hung airy vines.

The family greeted Charlie on the patio. Binh introduced his wife, Therese; daughter, Kim; and his son, Bao. Charlie's eyes went quickly to Kim. His mind was racing with many questions about each of the four, but he felt the importance of being respectful at this point and greeted them with a polite hello and a slight bow. "Good to meet all of you," he said.

It is interesting how first impressions are so enduring. Charlie had a good feeling for all except Bao. He was a tall handsome young man with intelligent eyes but had the body language of a twenty-year-old kid with a grudge against the world. The family seemed to ignore him. Later he would learn he had read Bao wrong.

Charlie felt nervous around the girl. She was completely foreign to anyone he'd ever known. He'd never talked to or been near anyone with such perfect natural beauty. At first he was uncertain if she was the same girl he'd seen unconscious at the track. She felt him stealing glances at her and smiled back.

After pleasant conversation, Binh said, "Kim, isn't it time you showed Lieutenant Strickland your horse?"

She answered that she'd been patiently waiting to do so, and with a pleasant smile gestured, "This way, please."

Chapter Five

Binh and Charlie followed her down a little stone path to the stable, which could hold up to four horses in box stalls.

As they walked, Charlie ventured a comment to Kim. "You look much better than the last time I saw you."

Nervously, Kim answered, "Oh! What a bad day that was! I still have a small bump on my head. It was all a blur to me … but I'm okay now!"

"I'm happy to hear that," he said as the three entered the barn.

Charlie saw the gray gelding standing in a box stall, its ears pricked forward. The big horse took an inquisitive step forward to see the visitors, which exposed his magnificent head carriage and very intelligent looking face.

"What a fine looking animal!" Charlie said as he stepped into the stall. He found the horse relaxed and carrying weight on the injured foot. Speaking in a low voice, he squatted down with his hand on the horse's left shoulder and then ran his hands gently down the big gelding's left front leg. He started from above the knee and carefully ran his fingers to below the pastern, feeling for any irregularities. Then he slowly coaxed the leg up and examined the hoof. The left hind leg showed a long scab that was healing well, obviously a scrape from the mishap.

Charlie thought the horse was doing well. "I'd guess he was lucky to escape with only a moderate ankle strain above the pastern. Perhaps a little more rest and light exercise?"

"My thoughts exactly," replied Binh. "I think he'll be good as new in a couple weeks. We are grateful you were quick to assist him on the track … could have hurt himself seriously."

Therese called to everyone that lunch was ready. As they walked to the house, Charlie was eager to talk more with Kim and could tell she had the same idea.

"I think you know horses," she said with a guarded grin, watching him askance.

"I think probably not as well as you."

"I mean, who jumps up from his seat in the stands and runs onto the track to untangle a horse in his harness?"

There was mutual laughter, and Charlie was relieved that Kim had such a natural good nature.

He said, "Didn't want him to suffer; thought he may hurt himself further. How did you know that anyway? I thought you were unconscious."

"Oh, yes, I heard, they told me all about it. You were the hero of the day, Lieutenant Strickland."

"Call me Charlie, my friends call me Charlie."

"Okay, let's see if you like my mother's cooking, Charlie!"

As they came into the house, Kim stopped Charlie and said, "Um … could I ask you to leave *that* here with the hats and shoes?"

She pointed to Charlie's .45 pistol. "My mother doesn't like them in the house."

"Of course." Charlie unbuckled the pistol belt and hung it in a small hallway right by the side door. Kim led him into a room that had a beautiful ceramic tiled floor. In general the house was very open, light and inviting.

Therese said, "We'll eat inside today, there's a nice breeze." Therese seemed to have a perpetual pleasant smile on her face. She led the group in the blessing before eating, the Catholic prayer, *Grace before Meals*.

"I see you are Catholic, also, Lieutenant," said Binh.

"Yes, my mother was Catholic, my real father was French, also Catholic. I was raised in the church."

Chapter Five

The five people began to enjoy Therese's cooking. The food was good, the company was good and the conversation was good except for Bao who was quiet most of the meal.

In fact, except for Bao, the conversation was lively. Binh talked about his ancestors being Catholic for many generations. And they were from the northern part of Vietnam, near Haiphong Harbor, not far from the China-Vietnam Border. When the country was divided into North Vietnam and South Vietnam by the Geneva Convention, many feared the Communist government would outlaw Catholicism as in the Soviet Union and China.

At that time, Binh's family decided to migrate south. He explained, "We left everything we had in 1954, and along with my two brothers and families we came to this area. The US Navy helped some two million people exit by the US Cargo ship, *USS Montague*. We were on that ship."

Kim spoke up, "I was only two when we moved and don't remember the north."

Therese spoke of her extended family's strength in their faith and how it got them through rough years in the late 1950s. They made good friends with a young French priest, Father Desjardins, who was associated with the new seminary at Nha Trang on the seacoast north of Saigon.

Father Desjardins helped them spiritually in their new life in the South, and they welcomed him to their home in Vietnam when he had time off from his duties. In fact, he lived with them for a number of months and was loved by the family. He told stories to the children of "Our Lady, the Star of the Seas." They were captivated by the mysteries and kindness of his seminary's patron saint. The family still corresponded with him in Paris, France.

Charlie could see the family was proud it was in contact with a priest in Paris. Binh made sure Charlie knew Father Desjardins was in an elevated position in the Church now. Binh was proud of his military experience also. He discussed his participation with the French Union Forces, explaining how Americans worked with the Vietnamese in intelligence gathering to support the war in the Pacific against the Japanese. "There were many alliances in those days against a common enemy, the Japanese," he said.

"Why, I wore these boots I'm wearing today when fighting with French Union Forces," Binh explained. "That's right, they were given to me by a French fellow fighter, and good friend when called back to France after the Japanese were expelled from Vietnam in 1945 and 1946. I retired from the ARVN in 1965 after being wounded near Kontum. That was when I was fighting with the Americans against the Communist insurgents. Now I'm a happy civilian with a medical retirement!" At that remark, all joined in light-hearted laughter except Bao who asked to be excused. He said he would be home late that night after work.

Charlie checked his watch and said it was time for him to leave, too. After he praised Therese for the lunch, Kim walked Charlie out the lane to meet Dao.

When they reached the end of the lane, there was no Dao waiting with the Bronco. Charlie was surprised. A little unusual, only because it was Dao. Charlie could imagine Dao now driving as fast as he dared, being upset that he was keeping his counterpart waiting "in the boonies."

Kim caught the concern in Charlie's eyes. "I'm sure your friend will be here soon," she said.

"Yes, I'm sure."

They sat down on a stone bench in some high grass near the abandoned French Colonial watch tower. "Let's talk," Kim said.

Chapter Five

This surprised Charlie, but he was anxious to ask about many things the visit had prompted, so he put concern for Dao aside for the moment. "I noticed two shrines in your house," he said.

"Yes, most Vietnamese homes have some type of altar or special place where we venerate our ancestors. We place pictures to remember them, in this place. Sometimes we burn joss sticks. You may have seen them at the altar. We bow before their images, thinking of them in a sort of spiritual way. You would probably call it praying. It's part of our Taoist religion. We are Catholic as you learned, so we have a little shrine to the Blessed Mother.

"Many Vietnamese believe it's not a conflict to honor one's ancestors with an altar, even though they are Christian. The shrine to The Virgin is my mother's doing. She is very strong in her faith and even uses her confirmation name, Therese, as her public name. She has been the force to keep our family strong spiritually. My mother has helped me greatly in supporting my education in Saigon, and I'm very grateful."

Charlie responded with, "You're very open about your life."

"Maybe direct is best ... most times."

"What about Bao? Is it just me that he avoids or is he always like this?"

"A little of both, I guess. As you saw, my father believes strongly in our democratic republic and hopes it will survive. Bao, not so much; he believes our leaders are corrupt. He went to Catholic high school like me and started University but dropped out recently because of many reasons, mostly money. Now he will have to go to the Army soon. He studied politics at University, and still meets with friends where they discuss the state of Vietnam. My father believes he could form a bad opinion of our republic. It worries my parents greatly, but Bao is very smart, and a little quiet, very academic. He's just curious about the world and all that's in it. I don't worry about Bao. He would never reject his country."

After a slight pause, she said, "I'm curious about you, Charlie, any family?"

"My mother and real father died years ago. My mother died in 1957 during the polio epidemic. I was ten years old so I have memories, good memories, of her. I don't remember my real father. He was killed in Europe shortly after WWII. My mom was working over there for the Defense Department at that time and they were married in France. He was killed in France a year or so later. I was only three years old in 1950, when my mom married a returning GI. He was older than Mom, but was a great father. He was a farmer. We had a dairy farm in the middle of Ohio. I loved it."

"So your father raised you alone?"

"Me and my sister, Brigitte. He was a good dad. Wasn't our real dad, but he always seemed that way to me."

"I'm lucky to still have both my parents," she said, then added, "How do you know so much about horses?"

"Oh, we had saddle horses on the farm along with cattle, Holstein cows." He chuckled. "Yeah, that was our hobby, my dad and me. We always kept a couple of horses. Dad loved them."

Charlie was surprised at her knowledge. They discussed other things and Charlie liked that Kim enjoyed good conversation. He checked his watch again. "Dao is nearly an hour late. Now I *am* concerned."

"I need to go back to the house, Mother will be worried. I'll come right back if you're still here."

A few minutes later, Kim came running up the path. She'd changed into casual clothes and had a look of urgency, "There's been trouble with your friend."

"You mean Dao? What kind of trouble?"

"He's been arrested."

"Arrested? Where? Why?"

"Yes, police have him in Can An."

"How do you even know this?"

"My brother Bao. He called my father. Bao knows some guys over there. I guess Dao had no I.D. Bao said the police chief is not trustworthy. He confiscated your truck."

"Oh! That's not good."

Charlie began to think. *How far was Can An? How long would it take him to get there? How much time before dark?*

"Charlie … I think Bao can help you."

Kim explained that Bao had a friend named Mi, who worked in Can An. "The chief probably wants a bribe. Bao said Mi's seen it before. But you're from the US Command. The chief will probably listen to you."

"Where is Bao?"

"He's in Can An now, with Mi. Mi's family has connections, and he can probably get you in to see the Chief."

"How far is this place?"

"Only four kilometers away. There's not much time, though, this is February, and dusk is still early, maybe three hours until dark."

Charlie looked to the western sky—shadows were getting longer. Kim added, "You should be back in Saigon before darkness. These roads are not safe at night."

"And how do I get to Can An?"

"I can take you on our family's motorbike."

"You have this all figured out, haven't you!"

"It's no trouble."

Twenty minutes later they were motoring through Can An on a 1962 100cc Honda motorbike. The police station was in the center of the village, in a grand old building built by the French colonial government in the late 1800s. As they pulled up to the building Charlie recognized the Ford Bronco parked in a lot a half-block behind the building, and they parked the motorbike there.

They met Bao and his University buddy, Mi, in front of the old building, adjacent to the village park. The afternoon was getting late and the few shops were closing soon. Bao's friend Mi had talked to the chief's secretary who had convinced the chief to see Charlie before the end of the day. The chief seemed to have agreed to the meeting as a gesture to Mi's family, held in high regard in the village.

Charlie thanked Bao and Mi for their help in setting up the visit. Bao, normally quiet, warned Charlie as he entered into the building: "Be careful, Lieutenant, this is his home ground."

Charlie nodded as he kept walking. Bao and Mi then slipped down to a local cafe to await the outcome of the meeting.

Kim accompanied Charlie as they climbed the stone steps. They passed through tall heavy wooden entry doors into a hallway, then into the open office of the district police chief. Kim sat inside the office door in a folding chair off to the side. Charlie's first impression was of a stark and dreary room. The chief sat behind a plain wooden table in the center of the back wall. A Republic of Vietnam flag hung from a pole next to the table. A framed picture of President Nguyen Van Thieu was mounted high on the bare wall behind, and handcuffs were hanging from a hook on the wall behind the chief.

An old French rifle case stood in a rear corner. Its door had been removed. Inside the case were two WWII French carbines, a 1950s sten gun and an M14 rifle. The chief, in khaki uniform and jungle boots, sat on a straight back wooden chair. Bright gold letters on a black background on a breast pocket read: *Bui Chi Bac, Police Chief.* Heavy eyelids nearly covered his gray-green eyes. His thin tight lips had a horizontal effect that lined up with his overall squarish face and jaw. Nothing about this man said friend of Americans.

"May I help you?"

Charlie started with a smile. "Thank you for seeing me, Chief. My name is Lieutenant Charles Strickland. I'm a US Navy advisor at the Vietnamese Navy Warfare Bureau in Saigon. I believe you are holding my counterpart here. His name is Lieutenant Dao."

"Please sit down, Lieutenant," he spoke in a lecturing tone.

Noticing Charlie's Navy Colt pistol, he switched to a patronizing voice and phony smile and said, "He disobeyed a traffic sign and my policeman stopped him. We gave him a warning, but he couldn't produce identification or registration for the vehicle, so we're holding him and the vehicle to protect the rightful owner."

Charlie felt his heart begin to beat just a little faster, and he took a deep breath. "The rightful owner is the US Navy, and I'm here to claim it."

The chief stared at him, but Charlie continued. "I'd like to see Lieutenant Dao now," he said.

"We are nearly closed for the day; it would be unusual to begin discussions with his case at this hour."

Charlie stood up. Chief Bui added, "But you may talk to him for a few minutes if you like."

"I'm afraid that won't be good enough, Chief Bui. You see, we need to return to Saigon tonight. We're both scheduled for a test run on a re-engined VN Navy speed boat early tomorrow morning."

The chief stood up, exposing a .38 revolver. Through a patronizing smile he said, "The moon and stars do not revolve around your wishes, my dear Lieutenant; you're under my jurisdiction now. I'll be here at 10 tomorrow morning to discuss the matter, if you wish."

The two men looked at each other, saying nothing for an uncomfortable ten seconds. Charlie thought: *How did this conversation go so badly so quickly?*

Finally Charlie said, "I thought we were on the same side in this war." He could feel his heart pounding.

The chief drilled his gray eyes into Charlie and said, "You know nothing of this war."

Charlie was pretty sure he and Kim and the chief (and, one hoped, Dao) were the only ones in the building, and he took a chance by saying, "Well, let me put it this way, Chief: I may not know much about this war, but I'm not leaving here without Lieutenant Dao."

He felt he owed Dao that much. He was now concerned for Dao's safety if he didn't get him out of here tonight. The two men stared at each other, daring the other to blink.

Charlie first felt the shock in the floor of the building, and then the pressure wave hit him an instant before the deafening explosion threw him into and over the chief's table. He lay in a pile of light plaster and could hear nothing as the smoke, plaster dust, and building debris rained down on him.

He was stunned for about two minutes, then got to his feet slowly and saw the chief under the table. His first thought was, *Where is Kim? I remember her sitting behind me.*

He looked around and saw her standing under an archway in the entrance with a cloth over her nose and mouth. She nodded and waved an arm to signal she was all right. The heavy entrance doors must have taken most of the blast, he reasoned. Assuming she was not hurt badly, he pulled the table off the chief then bounded up the flight of stairs to find Dao. Dao was on all fours, coughing and gasping for air. A portion of the roof covering the second floor was gone. Late afternoon sunlight shown through and beams of light caught the swirling dust, forming a dense fog effect. Visibility through the lighted dust was nearly impossible. Some of the walls of the cells were smashed. Dao got to his feet.

"Dao! You okay?"

"Yeah, okay. Let's get out of here! That mortar was meant for this building, so it's lucky it fell a little off. Let's go before the spotters get corrections to the gunners."

Charlie grabbed Dao by the arm and led him down the stairs, two at a time. They ran through the falling dust, jumping over blocks and ceiling beams and down the stone entry steps. They found Kim at the base of the steps, clearing the dust from her clothes and hair.

"Are you okay? Are you hurt?" Charlie said with alarm.

"No, just a little shaken. I can barely hear anything!"

"Me too!" he shouted.

Bao and Mi came running up from the cafe, and Bao shouted, "Hurry, we need to get cover; mortars usually come more than one at a time." He pointed down the street to a long deep concrete ditch townspeople used for a bunker.

Charlie thought: *Dammit! I should try to see about the chief,* and he said, "I'll follow you in a minute. I'm going in for the chief, if he's still alive."

"I'll go with you," Dao said.

The two of them ran back in and found the chief awake and sitting up but unable to stand or talk. He'd taken a major blow from the heavy table. Charlie shouted, "If you can hear, Chief, I'm pulling you out. We have to move quickly." They moved the chief onto what was left of the tabletop and began sliding him out. By the time they reached the top of the stone entrance, the town's first responders arrived and took over.

Charlie and Dao joined the others in the concrete bunker, relieved to see everyone safe. Less than five minutes later, as their hearing was starting to come back, the second mortar hit spot on and blew the rear of the building off. It was the largest explosion Charlie had ever heard and downright frightening to think he had just been sitting nearly dead center. After a few more minutes, Charlie looked up and saw Mobile Cav Hueys and began to relax a bit. He thought they must have located the source of the mortar. There was no third mortar and in thirty minutes, the "All Clear" sounded.

"I think the vehicles were far enough away to have avoided damage," Charlie said. "Let's hope your motorbike and the Bronco are okay."

Mi returned to his home. The rest stood together and watched the emergency workers. Bao was talking to the emergency warden and said, "There was no one else in the building. It was only the chief and us. They wanted to know who the American was."

Kim said, "Could we meet back at our farm and talk for a bit? My parents will want to understand what happened."

They found the vehicles only scratched up a bit from debris, so they headed back to the farm. The late afternoon light still held as they drove the few miles to the farm. Bao and Kim rode the bike; Charlie and Dao took the Bronco. They parked at the entrance to the lane, left the vehicles, and tried to shake the rest of the dust from themselves. Most of their hearing had returned. Bao said goodnight and began walking down the path to the house. Kim told Bao she would follow in a few minutes and join him to explain what happened. She sat down on the stone bench to rest, and Charlie joined her.

"Are you sure you're all right?"

"I'm not hurt, only a sore hip where some debris must have hit me." After a hesitation she said, "I was going to speak up, just before the mortar hit."

"But why?"

"To offer a compromise, Charlie," she said in a low calm manner.

"But why? Chief Bui was treating Dao unjustly; he should have released him."

"That's true, Charlie, but also irrelevant. I hope you don't think me too bold to say it, but you backed a proud man into a corner. Two men with guns arguing … not good. Too many good men shot and killed already. You left the chief with few options: only suffering a great dishonor or striking back with violence."

Charlie felt his blood pressure rise just a little but held his tongue and thought about what she said. He began to realize she'd seen things more clearly than he, and he said, "Well, you said you were direct."

Then he looked at her and more quietly said, "Okay, I get it."

"Oh, you guys must go now! It will be dark by the time you reach Saigon and these roads are not safe, especially tonight!"

"Yes, of course, but tell me, what do you think would have happened?"

"Oh, we were overtaken by events! It makes no difference now."

"Yes, but what if no mortars?"

"In that case, well, I don't know, maybe I would have tried to stop a fight; maybe I would have been too frightened."

"I'm thinking you may have been frightened but just brave enough to try."

"Could you blame me?" she said with a friendly smile. "I'm beginning to like you, Strickland. I didn't want to see you get shot. Now go quickly!"

Charlie began to turn away. He felt confused but kept going.

"Wait!" Kim stood up and walked toward him, stopped, and asked, "I know a lot happened today, but do you think we know each other well enough to be talking this way?"

He answered in a thoughtful tone, "I've known you for only one day, but I get the feeling you are just like you seem. Maybe like I'd somehow known you before. So … yes, I think it's okay."

She looked at him for a second or two, then said with an honest smile, "Yeah, me, too."

He walked slowly to the Bronco and stopped to look west. The sky was red, a deep reddish orange at the horizon that shot into streaks of pink across the world above them. To the north lay the immense flat Delta of darkening green and black, punctuated by thousands of wet paddies that now were even flatter mirrors of pink.

He looked across the land and thought: *I really don't know anything about this place, its land or people. But something happened today that made me want to know everything.*

Climbing into the Bronco, he and Dao headed back to the shipyard.

Chapter Six

New Boat Test

Charlie and Dao returned to Saigon just after dark when he dropped Dao at his home and drove to the shipyard. It was dark but not late. He took care of submitting his report to Captain Eagleton before he turned in. He played down the issues with the police chief. He knew Eagleton wouldn't want to know details, only results. The captain was always loath to become involved in "distasteful" matters with the locals. He felt it would reflect poorly on himself. Charlie focused on the mortar in his description of the event, and that they were all fortunate to be safe.

Before he retired for the night, Charlie wrote down everything he could remember about the incident, in case it came up later. He also made a note to himself to check on the police chief in a couple of days to close the loop.

Charlie had trouble sleeping that night, dreaming of his childhood horse, Black Martin. It was a reoccurring dream. He dreamt that he had forgotten to feed his horse for many days because he was busy with silly unimportant matters. He was shocked when he remembered at last, racing to the stall to find the poor animal suffering horribly and barely able to stand or to eat or drink. Even after he awoke, he was despondent for several minutes, still blaming himself. It was a dream he'd had since childhood. He rose and poured himself a small brandy and sipped it thinking of the day with the Binh family. He tried to examine how he felt about the visit and mostly about Kim. He felt bothered about how things were left when he drove off. He felt as though there was more he should have done and said when the opportunities had come up. Charlie wasn't sure how he felt about Kim, but he knew there was something different that attracted him. After an hour of sitting and thinking, he decided he should see Kim and the family again to learn more.

Charlie and Dao met early the following morning for coffee, and to go over the plan to test the upgraded patrol boat. As engineers, Charlie and Dao were anxious to fire up the new boat they'd been working on the last six weeks. Dao's sailors brought the boat to the research pier and gassed it up. Seamanship would be handled by four of Dao's sailors.

They took the boat out by way of the Saigon River. As they idled the engines, passing along the waterfront, they watched dock workers lined up along the wooden wharves and staring at them in the brisk morning mist. Charlie wondered what they were thinking as they stood there. The river was flat, flowing slowly. Even the bay was still as they moved out into the South China Sea. It gave Charlie time to think about all the things he didn't know about Vietnam and to resolve to learn as much as he could about the land and people without any preconceived notions. They speeded up and headed out to sea, motoring southward while keeping the shoreline within sight.

Chapter Six

Testing went well all the way to max design speed. The engine performed as intended. Dao was very happy with the improved performance. Both men reviewed the data and felt the testing was successful enough to begin planning for an endurance run to a base called Nam Can, on the southernmost tip of South Vietnam. They believed it would take about two weeks to organize and get prepared for the run down to Nam Can.

Chapter Seven

Eastertide Invasion

On the morning of March 30, Margot came waltzing through the office singing, "Somebody has mail." She dropped some letters on Charlie's desk (one was from Binh that Dao was forwarding) and winked as she passed by. I had to laugh the way she acted sometimes. Margot. What a great gal. You couldn't get her down. She was always in good humor; she never forgot a birthday. An American civilian two years out of the University of Notre Dame with a degree in international relations, her unwavering goal was an ambassadorship to some country in Europe—someday.

Margot was a good-looking young lady. She was friendly, single, and wanted it that way. Everybody in the office loved her like a sister. She applied for and got the position as Office Manager and Assistant to Commander, US Navy Technical Command, Navy Shipyard, Vietnam. It was a good starting point for the Foreign Service. She

Chapter Seven

had already written Navy summary reports and papers presented to Admiral Zumwalt, CNO (Chief of Naval Operations), and had been invited to meet him at a banquet at the Continental Palace in downtown Saigon. We heard he was impressed with her.

Margot announced, "Captain wants all hands meeting at 9 a.m., that means ALL hands, no excuses. Americans only." Charlie and I had just arrived for the day. I was heading out with my counterpart, Lieutenant Danh, to the town of Can Tho in the Delta, so we had to delay that.

Charlie said, "What's up, Margot? Why the meeting?"

"Captain will explain. Just know you should definitely be there."

Charlie and I grabbed a cup of coffee and moseyed into Eagleton's office where a number of folding chairs had been set up. Eagleton was at his massive desk. Margot was going over what looked like briefing papers and talking in a low voice close to the Captain. He sounded concerned and Margot seemed almost like she was trying to tone him down.

At precisely 9 a.m., he asked Margot to close the office door. She did so and sat down for the briefing. I looked around, only Americans were present and not even the vetted Vietnamese secretaries, which normally handled all the correspondence for the captain and Margot, when present.

Eagleton began, "I've asked all of you here this morning so you're aware of the official US Command communique on overnight military operations which occurred in I Corps (One of four military operational designated Core areas in South Vietnam; I Corps was the closest to the border with North Vietnam)." He read from a paper he was holding: "Early today the Peoples Republic of Vietnam Armed Forces launched an intentional cross-border attack on the Republic of

Vietnam by crossing the DMZ (Demilitarized Zone) at the 17th parallel with four divisions of the NVA (North Vietnam Army) troops supported by tanks and artillery. Their objective appears to be to seize the provincial capital city, Quang Tri. An additional two divisions of NVA troops attacked and moved toward Quang Tri from NVA bases in Laos. The attack has been met with resistance from ARVN units in the area. Quang Tri looks to be in serious danger of falling to the enemy from this surprise attack."

The Captain paused and several hands went up. He ignored them and continued without reading from the paper. "It's obvious since we have so few American combat units in Vietnam now that the ARVN will need to bear the brunt of this attack. It's likely that US Airpower will be involved. Our orders here in III Corps are to continue with business as usual, although it's likely that we will be limited in travel for our field projects because many of the aircraft we use will be diverted to bases up north for support. We'll use more ground transportation, if necessary. Also, our units working on new hardware designs to support operational units should continue those projects post haste."

Many in the room wanted to ask about planned liberty in the coming days but were reluctant to ask. The captain sensed that and said, "All liberty will be cancelled until we assess the threat in this area. Announcement on that will be forthcoming in the next few days, I imagine."

Most of those present were okay with the news, but Charlie was excited and couldn't wait to tell Dao. He immediately thought that because Quang Tri was on the coast there would surely be Navy armaments involved at some point. There might exist a need for the new boat design, and he thought, *It's a way for us to make a difference in this war ... however small it may be.*

Chapter Seven

Charlie asked, "Captain, will the VN Navy operational units be involved, sir?"

"It's likely the VN Navy as well as the US Fleet could play a role in this battle, in my opinion."

"What is the level of classification of the information you just gave us, Captain, sir?"

"No classification. It's for all-hands distribution."

That was it. Meeting was over. Charlie and I walked out of the captain's office discussing the news. As we passed Margot, Charlie said, "Nice briefing paper you wrote, Margot." She gave us a secret wink.

Chapter Eight

Escape at An Loc

Charlie had been in Vietnam for three months now, and things had settled down to somewhat of a routine. We were getting to know our counterparts well. Building trust and taking on riskier projects. We were due a couple days of liberty, and before the Quang Tri attack, the Captain had promised liberty for the coming Sunday. With the attack, we weren't sure about Sunday. I asked Charlie if he'd made any plans, "Binh invited me to the racetrack Sunday to see how the gray horse would run. I'll be on the infield at their holding area. Also, I heard he wants me to go with some of the family to evaluate a horse he's considering buying up around An Loc."

I teased Charlie and said, "With some of the family? As in with some *girl* in the family?"

"Well, I don't know exactly *who* is going. It all depends."

I told him more seriously, "Hey, I'm just sayin' … keep your eyes open, old boy. Don't get in too deep too fast."

Chapter Eight

Charlie's liberty plans came from a letter dropped on his desk that morning. It was becoming obvious that Binh thought a lot of Charlie and trusted his skills and his honesty.

After the briefing on the attack at Quang Tri, Charlie thought it may be tough to still get liberty on Sunday but sent a message back with Dao that evening that he would attempt to be there if he could. That was Friday, March 30. We all remembered that because it was Good Friday. It turns out that liberty was shut down through the weekend, but the captain opened it up starting Monday, one day for each person on a staggered basis.

Charlie drew Thursday, April 5, with the normal rules of checking in morning and evening. Charlie notified Binh who replied that Thursday would be fine. There was a minor race on Thursday, but it was actually a more convenient day to inspect the new horse Binh wanted to buy. As it happened, the fifth turned out to be an unlucky day for Charlie.

On Thursday morning, Charlie took a taxi from the shipyard and headed up Hong Tap Tu to where it connected with Plantation Road and the racetrack. Charlie arrived at the track at 10 a.m. The Binh family had arrived an hour before with two horses: the gray involved in the accident and a young filly in training to become familiar with the track. Charlie was delighted to see that Kim had come, but at first he felt nervous and awkward.

"Any remaining bruises from our last meeting at Can An?" he said, trying to make a joke.

Kim replied in a friendly and jovial manner. "Of course not, but let's hope we don't make our meetings so dangerous from now on!"

They laughed and did some small talk. Soon they were at ease, jabbering and comfortable to be with each other although it had been three weeks since the farm visit. They looked for chances to be together as they worked with the horses and prepared them for the track.

She explained that her father wanted to race the gray and had entered him in the first afternoon race at 1 p.m. but would evaluate him on the track first. If he wasn't ready, they would scratch him and enter the young filly they'd brought. Kim had already taken the horse for a half-speed practice run to test him, and Binh had waited till Charlie arrived for his opinion.

"I hoped you would be willing to ride him and let me know if you think he's ready," Binh announced. Charlie was surprised and honored that Binh trusted his opinion, and he hoped his old riding skills were still up to par. He mounted the gelding at once. The horse was all Charlie could handle, but after a few minutes of spirited trotting, he and the horse began to understand each other and Charlie felt comfortable enough to take him onto the track for a warm-up. A slow canter for a quarter mile and the horse wanted to go. He had an easy open gallop and Charlie was immediately surprised by his strength. He eased the bit and the horse responded with a burst of speed, but Charlie pulled him back for a restrained run for a good half mile. The horse wanted to run and he felt solid to Charlie so he let him open up for a quarter mile, then pulled him in.

Charlie let the gray cool down for a lap and brought him in to Binh's paddock. He dismounted and told Binh, "The horse feels solid to me. I think he's ready."

"Thank you for that, Lieutenant. That's what Kim and I thought, but we wanted to hear it from you." They untacked him and Kim and Charlie walked him around.

Kim said, "You know my father wants to buy a horse for sale near the town of An Loc. He's already examined the horse and likes it."

Chapter Eight

"And?"

"He wants us to check him out before he brings the horse down."

Charlie looked at Kim with a quizzical expression.

She shot back a little frown. "What?" she said.

"Nothing. I'm just amazed he trusts me to give opinions on his horses," Charlie said. "I'm not a veterinarian or anything."

"I'm amazed he trusts you to escort his daughter to An Loc and back this afternoon," she said. "Actually, I think he believes I'd be safer with you."

"I'm flattered ... I think. What do *you* think?"

"Oh, you seem the perfect gentleman," she said, smiling.

The horse raced at 1:30 p.m. in a field of eight good horses. The gray came in a distant second. All were pleased by his performance, understanding that having been off for a month he couldn't keep the speed up to close in the stretch.

Kim quickly changed after the race. Then she and Charlie left to check out the new horse. They took the motorbike and soon arrived at a small town about five miles south of An Loc, straight north on Highway 13. There they stopped at a small mom-and-pop place to grab a late lunch. It was about 2:30 p.m. when they arrived.

Charlie noticed some ARVN soldiers and military police in small groups around the town. He knew ARVN was on alert after the assault on Quang Tri, but that was way up north at the DMZ. He saw a US Army officer. The name on his fatigues read Captain Mathew Canon, MACV (Military Assistance Command Vietnam) Advisor. He was talking on an ARVN field telephone outside the restaurant. His call finished, Charlie asked him what was going on.

The young captain said, "Most of the guys you see around town are in our forward recon team. I'm their advisor. They sent us up here after some intel this morning that the area might be a launching point for another Eastertide invasion. We think there's a low chance of that, but we're doing some checking with the locals. We're near the Cambodian border here and a good place for a staging area to launch an attack."

Charlie looked at the small map he kept in his cargo pockets and noticed that the farther north they traveled on Highway 13, the closer they came to the Cambodian border. Captain Canon went on, "The information came from informants around An Loc and Loc Ninh. Could be the NVA is staging weapons somewhere over there in those jungles." He pointed to the west.

Charlie said, "We're heading north to a farm near An Loc. Do you figure it's safe five miles or so up this road?"

"Can't say for sure yet, but sometimes local fresh intel is good. My advice is do your stuff straightaway and head back south soon as you can. Don't linger. Ya' never know."

Charlie and Kim talked the situation over and agreed to go ahead and locate the farm, check out the racehorse quickly, then head back as soon as they could. After a quick refreshment, they gassed up the Honda and got back on the road.

It was now mid-afternoon, the weather was bright and sunny, hot, but not yet uncomfortably so. Charlie was driving, Kim sat side-saddle on the rear which was the custom. It was about as pleasant as it got in Vietnam. They clipped along on the Honda. The thirty miles per hour provided a pleasant breeze. Palm trees lined both sides of this section of Highway 13. It was a well maintained highway with dikes adjacent to the highway and paddies beyond. Kim lay her head against Charlie's back. He felt a surge of excitement her resting against him and knowing she felt comfortable in doing so. They passed An Loc and were quickly approaching the location of the farm.

Chapter Eight

With no warning, all hell broke loose. As they approached a crossroad and a small settlement of houses pushing up against an industrial area, artillery came screaming in. To the west and forward of them large explosions were suddenly occurring before their eyes. Some of the shells were dropping in the industrial zone immediately ahead of them. Horrific noise and smoke filled the air. He slowed the bike to miss debris on the roadway, and a deafening shell exploded in the highway ahead of them. He steered the bike as best he could off the road, scraping palm bark from a tree with the handlebars as the bike plunged down a slope by a paddy dike.

They came to rest in a water-filled ditch, the bike in the mud. Charlie turned and found Kim had fallen off as the bike stopped abruptly. He helped her up and they scrambled for cover in the ditch to assess their predicament. They were both somewhat shaken up but nothing serious. Charlie looked at the bike. The handle bars were bent and the left-hand controls had been wiped off. The front wheel was mangled. The bike was not ridable and would need serious repair work.

He looked across to the west and saw in the distance large military vehicles moving parallel to them across an open field at a tree line. Two of the houses in the settlement before them were burning and some kids had come running out and took cover in a small ditch beside the crossroad. North of them, up Highway 13, artillery shells were still falling.

Charlie first thought it was an ARVN military training session gone very wrong. Then he thought there was no way heavy shells would be thrown into an industrial area. And what about heavy military vehicles? ARVN would not be moving a line of what looked like Russian T-54 tanks into this area! This attack must be coming from across the Cambodian border.

They couldn't stay where they were. The farm they were seeking was probably no more than two or three miles to the east. Charlie said, "We need to get out of here quickly; we'll have to leave the bike. Maybe we can get help from the people at the farm."

They scaled the paddy dike and began to travel across country. Slipping and sliding in the mud at the paddy water's edge, they half-walked and half-jogged along the paddies in a northeast direction, staying on the cover side of the paddy dikes. By this time, the afternoon was beginning to heat up. It was so exhausting they both slid and fell several times. Charlie's boots began to load up with mud until they were so heavy forward progress was nearly impossible. Kim was struggling, too.

"Kim! Wait! Come here, sit down. Give me your foot," he said, between deep breaths. Her leggings were soaked and her riding boots heavy with mud. He carved more than an inch of mud off her boots. Trying to move quickly through the terrain while staying low continued to be exhausting. Kim slipped and fell; Charlie was forced to drag her up the bank out of the water. They both lay there a few minutes to rest, then continued, soaked in muddy water and sweat.

After forty-five minutes, they seemed clear of the shelling. They stopped and collapsed on the dike where a provincial road crossed a small canal, finding cover under a small bridge. Charlie took the opportunity to study his small map, and he located their position. "We're in luck: the farm is on this road about half a mile east."

They reached the farm by late afternoon. Wet, muddy, and exhausted, they trudged across the provincial road at the opening of the farm property. The farm buildings were across a field of low vegetation from a campus of abandoned large brick and block buildings.

Charlie sensed a familiarity with the area. "I've seen this place before ... I was here with Dao on a parts run three weeks ago," he said. "It's the same place. We passed through here but from another direction. We were in Phu Cuong and stopped to eat somewhere around here. It's an abandoned 'rec center' built for the French Legionnaires in the 1930s. It was a place of respite for the French soldiers, a break from the war. It's not a military base, per se, although they kept a small force here. It was close enough to the pacified areas to be safe. Dao said it fell into disrepair in the fifties when everything started to fall apart for the French. It's an interesting place. There's an Olympic-sized pool here and hotel-type lodging. Also, I see what look like tennis courts under the weeds and a large sports building. Everything is now overgrown and non-functional. The pool was all in-ground at one time, but the ground water in this area was too high and over the years it's pushed the pool upwards. It now sits partially above ground, lop-sided. There's a foot of rain water filling the pool's deep end. Lots of poured concrete in this place, if I remember."

The farm buildings looked small compared to the big structures in the rec complex. They checked but found no one at the farm residence. They entered a large barn where Kim could sense and smell horses. Coming from bright sunlight into the dark barn kept her from seeing clearly for a few seconds. As her sight returned she called to Charlie, "Wow! Look at this horse!"

Before her stood a tall racehorse, a true deep black color with no other markings. "I can see why Father is interested in him, a magnificent animal. We've never owned such a fine horse." She watched the big animal closely, his noble head high as he patiently observed the visitors. He was stabled next to a slightly smaller chestnut filly in a separate box stall. The chestnut seemed about the same age. Both animals were in good flesh, well cared for, and quite comfortable in the cool and dark partially stone block barn. Their feed bunks were filled with fresh orchard grass hay.

Kim reached up and checked his mouth. "He is three maybe four years old. I'm sure he's the one we're searching for." The slightly smaller chestnut filly seemed about the same age as the black. The horses had been fed, but the water trough was dry. Charlie searched and found that a pump had been rigged to one of the rec center's deep wells. They filled the water troughs and the horses buried their noses in the cool clear water and drank leisurely. Charlie and Kim splashed water on their own faces from the spigot and took gulps of the cool water with their cupped hands.

They sat down on a bench near the horses to rest and think. "The area seems to be safe from that shelling," he said, "but the owners must have believed the invaders were near and left quickly."

Suddenly the horses became alert and raised their heads. They stood still as statues with ears pricked forward toward a low rumbling noise. "Quiet," Charlie said as they both moved through the dark stable toward the side nearest the rec center. "Tracked vehicles, diesel engines," Charlie said. They peered out through gaps in the siding and saw the top half of a T-54 Russian tank on the far side of the old rec center.

"Dammit! I thought we had them behind us." He turned to Kim. She sat quietly staring at the tank moving slowly onto the main road of the rec center. Her mood had changed. It was not fear in her eyes but sadness, as if this was the beginning of the end of South Vietnam.

She spoke quietly. "Those tanks and soldiers are NVA forces. This is the first time I've seen them on our soil. Father said this day would come but hoped it wouldn't be in his lifetime."

"Now hang on, let's don't count the ARVN out just yet. The NVA attacked in Quang Tri last week, and the ARVN are up there blocking them with great courage. I'm sure they'll stop them here as well. Let's think positively," he said earnestly, with a smile.

"Yes, we should be thinking about our own plan of escape."

Charlie was watching from slits in the barn siding, and said, "There's a small company of men with those tanks. They seem to be setting up in the rec center. We need to lie low, stay under cover. There's no way we can leave now. We'll be spotted for sure. We'll have to wait until dark. We need to find a good hiding place in this building somehow. They are sure to nose around in this farm before too long. We are fortunate it's fairly dark in here, and a good deal of vegetation between us and the center. We may be able to hunker down quietly in here and wait for darkness. It should be dark in about three hours' time."

Kim had gone into the box stall and was quietly patting down the black. She whispered, "Charlie, this seems a wonderful horse, very gentle, exceptional conformation. I would be surprised if he wasn't fast." She proceeded to examine the chestnut and found it to be strong and gentle as well, although about half a hand shorter than the black.

He joined her and looked closely at the two racehorses. *It's true*, he thought, *good specimens*. He stood there studying the horses and thinking, then slowly turned toward Kim, who was watching him. Kim's mood had changed. She looked engaged in the moment, with a confident and determined smile. Charlie said, "Are you thinking what I'm thinking?"

"Exactly."

"We'll tack them up while it's still light."

"Yes."

"Bridles only."

"Yes."

"Exit out the big south door?"

"Yes."

"Do we mount before we exit?"

Kim instructed, "Absolutely not! Never mount a horse in the stable! Besides it will be quieter if we lead them out to the road."

"Right. Are we horse thieves?"

"No. First, we're checking out a horse we're considering for purchase. If we like him, we'll buy him. Second, I don't care, and I don't think you do either." Low level chuckles.

"One more thing: Are we stealing the chestnut filly?"

Kim whispered her response, "No, the chestnut and the black are friends, and don't like to be separated." Suppressed nervous chuckles.

Kim said, "Now shut up and let's find a hiding place."

"Agreed." More suppressed nervous chuckles.

They found a place between some stacked lumber on the rec center side of the barn and covered it with a canvas tarpaulin. There was an exit on both sides of the hiding place and enough room to stretch out. There were slits between the siding boards to watch the activity while daylight existed, but trying to see two hundred meters through the dark would be impossible. Sounds coming from the rec center earlier were quite audible, which was an advantage. The tall sliding door on the south side of the barn was wide open. This would be the obvious place to exit and make their get-away. They got busy and harnessed the horses with the bits and headstalls hanging outside each of the stalls. The horses took the bridles willingly. The horses would not like the bits in their mouths when attempting to eat or drink, but the two travelers didn't have much choice; they had to be prepared to move quickly.

The sun was sinking in the west and it would soon be dusk. Kim and Charlie were nervous and attempted to watch and listen from their hideout. All was quiet, except for what seemed to be movement of equipment and munitions into the area around the rec center.

Chapter Eight

They watched in the dusk as the tanks moved into and under the trees for what Charlie believed was cover from aerial observation.

The waning sun gave way to purple dusk. After that it was quiet. Without the sun it began to cool down. They lay down in their secret cave to rest and listen. Charlie pulled out his .45 Navy pistol and checked it. This was the only weapon between the two of them. He checked his ammo: two extra clips on his holster belt. He laid back against some grain sacks satisfied he'd done all he could to prepare. It was still and then Charlie heard what might be sobbing.

"Is that you in the dark?"

"Yes."

"Are you all right?"

"Yes, I'm just praying."

He thought for a few seconds. "Who are you praying to?"

"My favorite saint, St. Mary Magdalen; for our safe return, of course."

"So you're a true believer." And after a few seconds, "You believe in all of it. Communion of saints, forgiveness of sins, and so forth?"

"I do."

"I admire you for that."

"Why?" she said.

"Because I want to believe. It isn't that I don't believe at all, but my faith has faded. My mother had such a solid faith, and so did my real father, I'm told. My belief began to fade when my mother died." Charlie hesitated, then continued. "I just couldn't feel the closeness to the Holy Spirit that the church fathers talk about when I prayed for my mother and stepfather to recover before they died. Nor when my sister Brigitte was left immobile after the accident. I couldn't connect or feel that someone was listening."

"I think belief fades naturally in times of deep stress, if no one's keeping it alive with you. I've been lucky; my mother and a nun, a close friend nun at my school, were there for me in those times. Maybe you had no one, Charlie." Pause. "We can talk more sometime if you want."

"Yes, maybe. It's strange but I haven't talked with anyone like this about faith for a long time."

"You will be okay; you want to be."

After that it was dark in the barn. For twenty minutes now they had been lying quietly in the darkness of the horse building. They were pushed up against the side of a stack of lumber only one and a half meters high. A section of the roof in this area of the barn was missing, and through the tear in the tarp one could see only night sky above, illuminated by millions of stars. The night was cool and very still, no sounds except the low voices of the NVA Regulars out in the distance somewhere. It was difficult to judge their distance. Charlie reasoned it was quite far by the faint sound of their conversations, which seemed light-hearted with occasional laughter. He assumed they didn't know he and Kim were hiding there.

In the darkness Kim spoke out. "Charlie ... what is happening between us? I feel my life is changing, since you came. Maybe in your life, too. Do you feel it also?"

"I'm not sure what I'm thinking or feeling right now. Frankly, I'm still trying to sort it all out: the war, my place in it, this country, these people ... and ... even you."

Silence.

After another twenty minutes passed, Kim was restless and asked, "Why did you come to Vietnam? Of course the Navy sent you, but you must have had other options, right?

Chapter Eight

"Of course, I had other options. I joined the military for a lot of reasons, though I didn't expect to come to Vietnam. I was bored with my job at the University, and you know my real father was a Frenchman that served his country during World War II, in France and even in what we then called Indo-China. That's how my mom met him in France. I think I was pulled by that to serve, too. I felt it somehow honored him.

"I felt it was the thing to do. Many of my friends were in the military and actually were in Vietnam or had been here sometime in the 1960s. A friend was horribly wounded, not a close friend, but still someone I worked with. He will never recover. And I just wanted to see more of the world. I didn't want to spend my life regretting not serving in the military."

Kim asked, "Do you think this war will be over some day? Was it worth it? Is it worth all the suffering and death? Did you feel deeply?"

"You ask all the right questions." Charlie was quiet and deep in thought. "To be honest I was conflicted about that. I leaned to the side that trusted our country's leaders to do what was right. It was the honorable thing for our country to do, that is, come to the aid of people wanting to be free from communism. But now since I've been here, I don't know."

"Why?"

"I'm not sure it was all that honorable. I still believe South Vietnam has the right to choose their own government, but I don't think it's in the cards. The North wants to unify all of Vietnam, and the price to keep that from happening will be decades more of suffering and killing on all sides. Who am I to say what is right for Vietnam? I am beginning to believe we may have made a mistake in becoming involved. Though it may be right, it may not be possible. By the way, please don't tell anyone I said that, least of all your father! Ha!"

"Your secret is safe with me." Silence in the darkness for a few seconds, then Charlie felt her hand in his and a slight squeeze. "I'm thankful you came to Vietnam," she said.

A familiar noise broke the silence. The clinking of a tank's track links. The two peered through the deep dusk and strained their eyes to see any activity. A single tank had moved into position at the tree line and was facing the farm buildings. They both shivered. Then in the stillness, a single shouted order echoed through the canyons of the block structures. "Ban Ngay!" *(Fire Now!)* One second later, the tank fired a deafening blast that completely blew apart one of the small French-built block farm buildings. Nothing remained but a pile of rubble partially visible in the dusk as smoke from the direct hit cleared.

Kim said, "It's a test. They're trying to scare anyone in these buildings to run out. If we run out now we would be targets. It's a trick they use, like a hawk that screams a terrifying warning, and the prey moves to escape but in doing so gives up his position and the hawk dives for the kill."

Charlie asked, "How do you even know this stuff?"

"From Bao. The Viet Minh are trying to recruit him, and they tell him stuff like this."

"I don't think I want to know any more about your brother," Charlie whispered. "If you're right, they will probably send a man or two to walk around and through these buildings. If they spot us, we will have to move fast. There is a dirt path straight south out the big door. It connects to a narrow highway. Its name isn't shown on the map. We need to go left and east on that road for at least a mile or two before we go south. If we get that far, we should circle back sometime to pick up Highway 13 down south to head home. It's a long shot, but it's the only shot we have."

Chapter Eight

Kim said with confidence, "I don't think it's such a long shot, Charlie. Remember, I saw you ride that gray racehorse this morning; you're no slouch." Charlie turned and they looked at each other without speaking. A little smile slowly crept across his face and he said, "You know, you may be right; we may just make it out of here." They sat back to wait and listen.

In the silence a cracked bell clanged in the direction of the rec center, then stopped. Charlie said under his breath, "What the hell was that?"

Kim said, "It's from that tower by the rec center building. The French probably used it for morning Mass. There were a lot of Catholics in the French Legion ranks. Probably hasn't been rung in years. It could be another trick to confuse or spook anyone here to run."

"Can you mount the chestnut bareback without a step?" he asked.

"Maybe, but I doubt it. She's too tall."

"All right, I'll give you a leg up before I jump up on the black. We'll have to mount in the barn, we don't have a choice now."

Kim touched his arm and with her finger pressed against her lips motioned to a solitary figure silhouetted in the big door against the last of a dusky sky. The adrenalin surged in both of them as they silently absorbed the moment they had hoped wouldn't come. As the NVA soldier turned to look into the barn, Charlie whispered, "Judas Priest! The bastard's got a sten. One burst from that is all he'll need."

He pulled out the .45 and they began crawling as quietly as possible to their escape route opposite the soldier. The soldier entered the barn slowly and waved a flashlight around, saw the horses, and stopped. Charlie was thinking, *He'll see they're tacked up and know something's up.* The horses became restless and they fortunately masked any noise as he and Kim stood up, still hidden behind the lumber but now out from under the tarp. Their hearts were pounding as they readied themselves for what the next few seconds might bring.

As predicted, the NVA trooper probed farther into the building and came toward their hiding place. For a moment he was silhouetted against the door opening, which fixed his position. He was only ten feet from them when his light beam caught Kim and he shouted, "Dung Lai!" (*Halt!*) As he swung the sten into alignment, Charlie shot him once in the chest. The Navy colt broke the stillness like a cannon. The soldier dropped to a knee then fell backwards. Charlie dropped down and checked him with the light. He was dead, shot in the heart. He looked closer and dropped the light.

"Oh God in heaven!" he said. "He's just a kid. I shot a young kid!"

Kim put her hand on his shoulder. "You had no choice, Charlie; you know that! Come on, we'll talk of it later, now we must move!"

Her voice was shaking but resolute. Charlie picked up the light, got up, and headed to the horses. He called back to Kim, "Grab that sten if you can; we may need it. There may be others lurking; we must go now. If we're lucky, we may have a few minutes."

Quickly he moved into the chestnut's stall, hoisted Kim up, and led horse and rider out. Then into the black's stall. The big horse was already excited by the gunshot and his stablemate being led out. Charlie talked to the black in a low quiet voice to sooth him, then mounted without difficulty.

"Do you have the sten?" he called.

"On my back, Charlie! Let's ride!"

They shot out the big south door and down the path toward the highway. Kim led the way crouching low, true to the professional she was, with the light-weight sten strapped across her back. Charlie's legs were clamped tightly around his barebacked horse. He grabbed a handful of thick black mane in his left hand and the reins in his right. It was obvious he lacked the riding skills of Kim, but he was confident in his ability to handle the black, though it might not look pretty.

They pushed their mounts into a full gallop down the earthen path as a pale moon rose behind a ghostly thicket of thin clouds. The rush of cool air at speed and the sound of pounding hooves beneath them on solid earth sent a chill through Charlie. He had never felt such adrenaline and wild swirling emotions. When they swung onto the highway, they heard the clatter of AK-47 fire somewhere behind them. The riders crouched lower and stretched the racers out into a full run as they ran a midnight race by moonlight down the narrow deserted highway.

The black caught up with the smaller horse quickly, and Charlie glanced over with a look of confidence in the girl who raced horses. *What an incredible and beautiful woman*, he thought. Flying through the night like a spirit of the wind, her dark hair streaming behind her and the moonlight lending a luster to her face the color of white gold. She rode as though she was attached to the animal, low and forward, moving in one beautiful fluid unified motion of horse and rider. The chestnut's withers became her saddle pommel while her knees were clamped loosely on the animal's cycling shoulder muscles. Charlie would remember this sight forever. She returned the look with a smile of gratitude and trust in her new partner amidst the raw reality of a horrifying war.

The animals were breathing heavy now and beginning to lather as they put more and more distance between themselves and danger. After another half mile they slowed the horses, and as they began to sense the triumph of escape a slow release of tension transitioned into euphoria. Kim gave Charlie a smile as if to say, "I told you so!" They took the first provincial road south, travelled along a dike pathway and finally connected to Highway 13 and headed south and homeward.

They walked the horses down the highway, trying to cool them and to look for water. The highway was quiet which was not unusual for this time of the evening. Somewhere in the area south of Lai Khe they came upon an ARVN outpost consisting of a couple of small block buildings around a former French stone tower that held an RVN flag and surrounded by a small grove of banyan trees. They were approached by perimeter sentries with M16s while a US Air Cavalry spotter flew high overhead. They stopped and found there were two American advisors at the post. Charlie and Kim slid off their mounts. Their legs and backs where horribly cramped. Kim put her arm around Charlie's waist for support, looked up at him, and said, "We did it!"

Charlie looked down and smiled at her, then pulled her close in a full embrace. "Yes we did!" he said.

An American Lieutenant saw Charlie and queried, "Where in the hell are you guys coming from!? What are you doing out in this dark night on two horses? Late date night, Lieutenant?!"

"Not hardly."

Charlie explained what happened on their trip, which was supposed to be the inspection of a horse north of An Loc. The lieutenant told them US Command had already been informed about the incursion and artillery attack.

"Come daylight, this whole area will probably be on fire. Got a feeling US Command will move the big guns in with Air Cavalry." Then added that the recon force was ambushed and had been wiped out near Loc Ninh. Charlie was shocked, "No! Did the American captain make it?"

Chapter Eight

"Sorry, Lieutenant; everyone. Everyone was killed."

Dejected, Charlie turned away and said, "Can we get these horses some water?"

"Sure, Sergeant Mau can do that. He likes horses."

Charlie found Kim sitting on a rude bench built against a temporary fortification of sandbags situated between the old French tower and a large banyan tree. Kim was quiet, looking into space. She seemed to be assessing the day, deep in thought. She was sitting in the mostly dark, except for a lantern light that played on her weary face and eyes that reminded Charlie of the human element that continued to be scarred in this war.

A transistor radio had picked up an Armed Forces station in Saigon and was playing at a low level the popular song in Vietnam, "So Far Away" from the album *Tapestry*. Charlie thought: *How far away and perhaps insignificant was America and home tonight.* Two VN soldiers ate a late supper after their watch. Charlie could smell the nuoc mam and asked Kim, "Are you hungry? The officer said we could eat if we want."

She shook her head without talking. She seemed to be in a trance.

"You should at least have something to drink. There's water or tea in those pitchers."

"I'll have some tea in a minute."

Charlie went to the pitchers and poured two glasses of tea. He handed one to Kim and sat down beside her. He was physically and emotionally worn out, and he knew she was, too. "The lieutenant said they have good communications here. You should call your family. I'm sure they're worried. Maybe they've heard about the attack. You know bad news travels fast. They said they can hook up to Tiger Central Telephone Exchange. You could call your father. We need to do something about these horses tonight."

The thought of the horses seemed to break her spell. "Yes, you're right ... okay, good, I'll call him. What shall I tell him?"

"Why not tell him exactly what happened ... everything."

"Yes, everything, I'll tell him everything. I'll tell him we escaped on the horses, and you saved my life and ... "

"Yes, you tell him I saved your life and I killed a kid in doing so!"

Charlie stood up. "What a night! They killed young Captain Canon ... I killed an NVA kid soldier. Tit for tat. Nothing changes. What the hell is the sense in all this?"

Kim said gently, "Charlie, you did what a good man does. We will talk of those things later. Tonight let's just deal with the things at hand."

Charlie took a deep breath and said, "Yes, I know, it's just that I can't stop thinking about that kid. You go ahead call your father. I'll call Margot in Saigon and let her know where I am. I'll file my report in the morning."

Kim got through to her father and found he was at the track. She found Charlie who had just finished talking to Margot. "Father is coming here; he's at the track. He has the track's farm truck and trailer and wants to bring the horses to the track overnight. He's bringing Bao with him."

"Bao?"

"Yes, Bao to help him ... don't worry, Bao will help. You'll get to know him better ... he's not a bad guy."

"Does your father know where we are? Near Lai Khe?"

"He knows the place. We're only twenty miles from the track. He passed here when he checked the horse, remember? We can ride back with them to Saigon. They'll be here in thirty minutes."

"Wow, you've got it all handled ... as usual," he said soberly.

Chapter Eight

When Binh arrived he went to his daughter and embraced her for a long time. "So thankful you're safe." He was shaking with emotion. To Charlie he said, "Once again I am in your debt, Lieutenant."

Charlie replied, "Thank you for that, but it was a combined effort that saved us today. Kim had the confidence we could escape by horseback, and we did. And I must say we gave those horses a good checkout! They are damn good sound horses!"

Binh and Bao loaded the horses and they all headed back to the track. The truck cab had room for only two, so Charlie and Bao rode in the truck bed. When they got going, Bao asked what happened.

"Pretty simple, we walked into the path of an invasion of an NVA unit from the Cambodian border. We ran and hid in a barn around An Loc somewhere. A soldier found us, I had to shoot him to escape. We eluded the NVA by getting away on the horses that were stabled in the barn. We circled south finally back to Highway 13. Sorry about your motorbike. It's toast. It'll need some major work to put it back on the road."

"It was a surprise, huh?"

"Surprise?! Well, hell yes, it was a surprise!"

Charlie was feeling testy but realized later there was no call to bark at Bao, who was quiet the rest of the way to Saigon.

They dozed for twenty minutes. The truck stopped and Charlie woke up on Hai Ba Trung Street in Saigon where he'd asked Binh to drop him. It was 10 p.m. Kim slipped out the passenger door. Charlie checked the horses and saw they were all right and met Kim.

"I'm going to pop in to Joe's place a block down the street here and see if he wants to grab some food. I'll get a taxi home tonight."

Kim was looking down and said, "Thank you for everything today, Charlie. I guess our family sure got you into a mess today."

He grabbed her hand and said, "Hey, we made it through okay, didn't we?"

Both did their best to check emotions that were now on fire. Neither wanted a scene in front of her father. She continued, "We can maybe meet in a few days? We still must talk of what happened, and try to make sense and what it means … I know how you feel … you talk to Joe tonight; he's your good buddy."

Charlie smiled and a nodded. "Yes, you and I will meet soon."

Her father came around the truck, and in front of her father and with no inhibitions she slowly and deliberately reached up and put her arms around Charlie's neck. She pulled him close for several seconds, then kissed him on the cheek, and whispered, "Thanks for saving my life today, Charlie Strickland."

The only words Charlie could get out were, "Anytime kid," and a quiet, "Goodnight, Kim."

Chapter Nine

Beers at Kenny's

Charlie did show up at my BOQ that night in early April. He'd banged on the guard shack to get the attention of the Chinese guard who had fallen asleep. The guard called me and I met Charlie out front. In the dim street light he looked like hell.

I said, "Margot told me about the trouble you guys had today. I'm relieved to see you made it. You look rough, man."

"Yeah, I feel rough. The worst was I had to kill an NVA bastard to avoid us being captured or worse. We escaped on horseback; on the horses we found in the barn."

"Where's Kim, is she here?"

"No, with her Dad. He met us south of Lai Khe. He's got the horses in the trailer. They'll keep them at the racetrack overnight. He dropped me off up the street. Hey, listen, I'm starving. I need food and drink. Want to grab something up at Kenny's American?

I need to talk through about what the hell happened. Let me clean up a bit first."

"Sure, come on up. I'll grab my wallet and we'll go." A few minutes later we walked into Kenny's. Kenny's American Bar and Grill was over on Dang Duc Sieu, down the street from the old US Officer's BOQ, now decommissioned and pad-locked. Josie was tending bar to a near empty place that quiet Thursday evening. Kenny was working the grill. It was a no nonsense bar. No fights, no monkey business. Lots of unit insignias like 1st Cavalry Division, Screaming Eagles, 23rd Infantry Division, and Seabees MCB-4 hanging on the walls and behind the bar. Kenny himself was a disillusioned Vietnam vet who had met Josie when she was a teenage "Saigon tea girl." She hustled GIs for overpriced drinks—and a little extra if the tips were good. That was back in the mid-'60s before the TET Offensive.

He and Josie had been a couple since back then, when they were young and a little crazy. Kenny's uncle had sent him $250 in 1965 to come home, but Kenny and Josie used the money to start a bar. They found success immediately. They'd been together now six or seven years. Both had grown up a lot in that time. They'd settled down into a kind of career and even started to look and act like an old married couple. Almost a bit of normalcy in the whirling tide of Vietnam. I liked the way they treated each other. With respect. A good couple. I once watched Kenny cold-cock a sailor who'd made a slur at Josie. The rest of the patrons dragged the sailor out. That's how much they respected the couple.

"Me and Mrs. Jones" was playing on the juke box, and a very young tea girl was sitting next to a US Army colonel at a small table. The colonel was fixated on a story in the *Saigon Post* evening edition. She had her hand on his leg, trying to coax a tip from him. He was paying no

Chapter Nine

attention to her. There were two US ex-pats sitting at the bar, discussing a bridge repair project somewhere in the Delta.

Josie turned and smiled hello as we walked in. Kenny said, "What'll it be fellers?"

"Two 33 Exports, please … large ones."

"Food?"

"Two cheeseburgers, American."

I said, "Make it just one. I'm not hungry."

Charlie said, "Negative, I'll eat both."

Josie brought the beers. Charlie was thinking hard as he poured his beer slowly from the green bottle into his glass. He watched the bubbles rise and turn into a frothy head. He took a long slug then looked at me and said, "It feels good to sit down and decompress. I am totally wasted."

I told him I couldn't believe that Margot came over after she updated the captain when you called in.

"She actually came over? I'm impressed. Good old Margot. By the way she's been laying big eyeballs on you!"

"Stop it. Never happen, GI." Then after a few seconds: "You shot an NVA guy and escaped by horseback? Now that's something I wasn't expecting to hear about your day of liberty. She also said you were caught in an artillery barrage."

Charlie looked at me and said soberly, "Yeah, it's hard to even believe it all really happened; like a bad dream. It was my day of liberty. I spent most of the day trying not to be scared shitless, which I was. Margot must have forgotten the part where I wrecked their motorcycle and left it in the mud." Weak chuckle.

"Margot said the captain will want a report tomorrow."

"Of course, I can do that," Charlie said absentmindedly. Kenny put the cheeseburgers in front of them, "Here you go, fellers."

Charlie took another swig of beer and said, "There's something else. Remember when you told me to be careful of getting in too thick with things? Things of course meaning Kim?"

I nodded.

"Well, I'm in deep now. You're probably the only one I know who'd understand this."

He took a bite of his burger, chewed it up slowly, and swallowed it. He started talking in a low thoughtful way. "Just an unbelievable day. It was down to the most basic levels of life and death. We just struggled to stay alive together. That's what it amounted to. Trying not to die."

"How did Kim take all this?"

"Kim? Kim was cool through it all."

Charlie began talking slower and became more distant. "We were so damn worn out trying to get away from those bastards. That's the main thing I remember, being so damn tired. Running east, trying to get away from the artillery. And down in the mud and the sweat. The sun was hotter than hell up there around An Loc today. Kim was soaked from stumbling and falling into the paddy water, and covered with mud from running along that dike.

"At one point I pulled her out of the water, or should I say *dragged* her out, crawling myself. She had rolled into deeper water and I was trying to keep her face above water while dragging her out. You know, so she could breathe. There was no pretense, we were down in the mud and water, but she was real game."

Charlie shifted his train of thought and continued, "I never really expected to kill a person, though I knew it could be a possibility over here. I had no idea how I'd feel with my own death imminent. I was scared as hell. The NVA guy was up close. Aimed his sten at us. For just an instant, it was him or us. Simple as that. So I shot him. Couldn't

Chapter Nine

possibly miss. Too close. One shot, *blam!* He was just a kid. Fourteen, max. But he was going to kill us with that sten so I shot him. We both got sprayed with his blood. I didn't know he was a kid, but it wouldn't have mattered." He paused. "Same difference, us or him ... I had to do it."

Charlie stopped and searched for words. "Everything about it was so ugly. Bloody. Exhausting. That kid was so small and young. Makes me feel rotten." He stopped, took a deep breath, and let it out slow. He drank some more beer and was quiet for a while. Someone must have played "Me and Mrs. Jones" again, for it was playing once more but at a lower volume. We drank some more beer and looked down at the table, in our own thoughts. It was quiet but not uncomfortable. After a couple of minutes Charlie started up again.

With a weak chuckle, he said, "The horses were the surprising thing. I never would have believed we'd get away on those horses. Too many things to go wrong. But Kim had total confidence. I trusted her, she said I could do it. She convinced me to try it. So we did."

Charlie looked like he was ready to wrap it up, and he said, "We kind of saved each other, I guess. We had to keep each other going. I can't imagine I'll ever get over it. Like I said, I'm in deep now." He paused. "I like her a lot, Joe." Pause for a few seconds. "I'm talked out, I need to eat and sleep."

I was relieved that he was ready to eat. Frankly, I was worn out myself just listening to his story. Charlie finished his cheeseburger, and we both drained the last of our 33 Exports. I sat and tried to think of how to respond to what he had just told me.

Finally I said, "It's good you spilled some of that out; maybe it will help some. It'd probably be good to see a chaplain or somebody more professional. Talk it through with them." Pause. "It can't be good to kill a man, but there's no question you did what was right. You're a good man, Charlie. You've got a good head and a good heart. I don't know Kim that well ... yet. Apparently you guys did what you had to do and made it through by relying on each other. I'll support you, whatever you decide ... you know, with Kim ... if I can."

"Thanks, man."

We paid Kenny and left with one cheeseburger still on the table. I saw the colonel suddenly pick up the *Saigon* extra edition, go over to the two guys at the bar, and say, "Did you fellas see what the hell happened up by An Loc today?"

We hailed a taxi and drove to the shipyard to drop Charlie off, then the driver swung up Hai Ba Trung and dropped me home. Charlie finished his report that night and hit the rack. He knew it would be a big day of questioning tomorrow but he was so wasted he didn't care and slept like a baby.

Chapter Ten

Meeting of the Spies

Charlie sought out Dao first thing the following morning to bring him up to speed on the trip to An Loc. He wanted to make sure Dao understood what had happened about the shooting of the NVA soldier, and that he heard it from him first. He also wanted to ask if Dao could get in touch with Binh or Kim to see if she would be free this week or perhaps would be at the track. Charlie knew he needed to talk with Kim. He wanted to talk to her about the escape and the killing. He knew they somehow needed to close the book on that episode. He also knew it wouldn't be today, thinking the captain would probably have him tied up in some way, debriefing his trip to An Loc.

Dao was ahead of the game. It turned out Dao's wife, Phuong, had introduced herself to Kim several weeks prior and had a budding friendship going. "Already got that handled, Charlie," he said. "Wednesday evening, 8 p.m. at the Piccolo bar on the Wharf. Phuong and I will be there, too."

"But how?" Charlie asked.

"My wife; seems she and Kim have been talking. I find it best not to ask questions. I've learned everybody's happier that way," Dao said with a chuckle.

"I didn't even know your wife knew Kim ... but good, that's great, thank you!"

Charlie was relieved that a dinner was set. He was also anxious to discuss the upgrade boat projects with Dao. He wanted badly to make some contribution to the war effort now that there could be an opportunity for their development team. This would have to wait a bit, though, as he found when Margot came waltzing down the hallway.

Grabbing him neatly by the arm and swinging him in a dance move to the reverse direction, she began, "Captain read your report and wants you in his office pronto."

Charlie grimaced and said, "Blast it, there goes my morning, and all I get is a few dance steps in three-quarter time!"

"Isn't that enough, you poor deprived soul? Can I get you anything for the meeting?"

"Yes, a copy of my report, a cup of very strong black coffee and ... two Hostess snowballs."

"Hey! If I had two Hostess snowballs, they'd be in the safe!"

Charlie knocked on Captain Eagleton's open door and this time the captain called him in immediately. "Come in and sit down, Strickland." Charlie stepped in then noticed a Navy intelligence officer sitting in front of the captain's desk, and Charlie's report was lying in the middle of the Singaporean desk. Margot brought in three coffees, along with another copy of Charlie's report and a stenographer's pad, then closed the door.

The captain said, "I've asked Margot to write the minutes of the meeting. This meeting will carry the security designation of SECRET;

we all have at least a Secret clearance in this room." The captain began, "Lieutenant Commander Brian Hargrove will be joining us today … from NISO (Navy Intelligence Service Office)."

"How are you, Commander; I recognize you from advisor training at Mare Island." Charlie acknowledged him in a friendly tone, but he was thinking, *Okay, this will be a real debriefing and probably all morning, at least.*

"Yep, I was there. Good to see you, Charlie, and call me Brian."

The captain continued. "Commander Hargrove will listen in, and we may have a proposal after we discuss your report. I must say it was one of the most unusual reports I've read in a while, Strickland. It seems quite complete. Is there anything else you'd like to add?"

"No, sir, can't think of anything else."

"Then the report will be submitted *in toto* as Addendum One to these minutes." The captain continued. "You obviously had a harrowing experience; we are of course glad that it wasn't worse and you made it back safely." The captain paused and looked down at the report in front of him. "Let me ask you, Lieutenant, how are things going in general with your assignment here?"

"Very well, sir. My counterpart, Lieutenant Dao, and I work well together, and we've recently made good progress on projects the team is working on. We sat down with VNN (Vietnamese Navy) Operations Group after the attack on Quang Tri to determine if there was an opportunity for us to quickly help the war effort up there. They believe that two of our projects would be valuable in making a significant difference: the High Velocity Skimmer (high power speedboat used for reconnaissance and close-in intelligence gathering), and the Heavy Duty Ferro Patrol Boat. We've made these two projects top priority now. The whole team of engineers and sailors that Dao leads is excited about being part of a real effort up there. Seeing their work going into military hardware that helps win the war has sparked a lot of enthusiasm."

"I'm glad to hear that, Lieutenant, that's good news."

"Thank you, sir."

The captain shifted in his chair uncomfortably and said, "I'd like to discuss another subject, which is the reason Commander Hargrove is here."

Charlie's engineering mind suddenly shifted and big red flags went up front and center.

The captain went on. "It's of course obvious from your report that you've been spending more and more time and becoming friendlier with those local native horse people. As you know, I've advised against that because it's a good source for trouble. But you have apparently ignored my advice. Well, it looks like that is exactly what happened: you got into a lot of trouble yesterday."

Charlie couldn't help pushing back and said in a respectful manner, "Captain, sir, the local Vietnamese had nothing to do with the trouble. I was on an authorized day of liberty in a US Command authorized area and was attacked by North Vietnamese shell fire and infantry!"

Raising his voice, the captain sternly admonished Charlie. "Please! Please, Lieutenant! Do not interrupt me!"

"Sir."

"As I was saying, you continued to become friendly with this family and especially the daughter. Well, Commander Hargrove has read your report and believes this could be of value to his intelligence unit."

Another legion of red flags taller than the first paraded across Charlie's mind's eye.

Charlie said, "Intelligence unit? I know nothing about intelligence work. I'm a mechanical engineer, for heaven's sake!"

Chapter Ten

The captain motioned to Hargrove as his entry point. "Commander?" he said.

"Thank you, Captain. First off, I'd like to commend Charlie on quick thinking and action on getting out of that fix you were in yesterday near An Loc. And second, I'm impressed with the work you and your counterpart Lieutenant Dao are doing. In my opinion, your quick response to shift priorities in the development group in response to the NVA attack is very admirable and right on the mark as far as what our advisor program is trying to accomplish."

"Thank you, sir."

"Charlie, in just a short time you've shown yourself to be one of our advisors with the initiative to become more knowledgeable of the country and one of the people who make things happen. I also read your report on the incident in Can An. It's another example of working together with the Vietnamese to accomplish something worthwhile. The Vietnamese seem to trust you and work *with* you instead of *for* you, as it happens in many cases."

Charlie said nothing but paid full attention, waiting for a shoe to drop.

The commander continued. "I'd like to share with you the fact that we have some information on the family that you've been seeing, that is, the family of Nguyen Binh Li, the racehorse trainer."

"What kind of information?" Charlie asked.

"What do you know about Bao, Binh's son?"

"Only that he's their son. Hardly said more than two words to him."

"We have some intelligence that he actually may be an informer for the Viet Minh."

"No idea, don't know that."

"Lieutenant, we'd like you to help us learn more about him."

"All I know is he helped us get an appointment with the police chief in Can An when Lieutenant Dao got arrested there for not having his driver's license with him."

Commander Hargrove went on. "What we mean is we'd like you to continue your relationship with this Vietnamese family and their daughter and to listen for and watch for any indications that this individual may show himself to be a sympathizer or perhaps even an active participant in a Viet Cong cadre. He could provide valuable information, through your observation, on upcoming enemy movements or plans that could save American and/or Vietnamese lives."

Charlie's blood pressure had been building quietly until finally he blurted, "So you want me to spy on this family! The family that just trusted me with the life of their daughter, and I trusted her with the plan to save our lives and it worked! Is that it?! Let's don't pull any punches here, gentlemen!"

Captain Eagleton said, "Now see here Strickland, you're speaking to senior officers! May I remind you that you took an oath to protect your country against foreign enemies. Your allegiance belongs to your country, and not to some third world gooks that we're bending over backwards for to save their own country because they are either too lazy or too cowardly to fight for themselves!"

Commander Hargrove interrupted. "Gentlemen, let's please tone down the rhetoric ... please."

Charlie began again. "Captain, Commander, this family is certainly not as you described, Captain, and denigrated by the racial slur. They are an educated middle class family that has worked hard and showed they are on the same side as we are. They are a respected family that has a long record of strong support for the Republic of Vietnam. They migrated from the north in 1954 and left everything to come here.

Chapter Ten

Binh himself fought in the ARVN many years, was wounded multiple times, and is on a disability retirement now, as I understand it. His wife, Therese, was a schoolteacher and has kept the family together for years while Binh was away at war. With the greatest of respect, I think you are barking up the wrong tree here."

The captain was about to launch into a diatribe that could have included the word *court martial* when the commander interrupted. "Excuse me, Captain, if I may." Then he went on. "Charlie, I apologize for the slur, I know even our advisor training disallows use of those terms, and I have to say your description of the family actually matches well with the information we have already. There is only one family member that is in question, and from your own observation you know little about him. We know he is secretive, and two days ago we know he made contact with a person we have verified from our sources as a member of a Viet Cong unit that was responsible for the burning of a least two villages. Villages that refused to provide materials and funds to the cadres. Several Vietnamese civilians were killed in that incident. We are only at this point trying to find out if Bao could be privy to plans, strategies, movements of the enemy, and so forth."

Charlie was quiet for a few seconds, then said, "Do I have a choice?"

Immediately the captain began to bellow. "Hell, no, you ... "

Hargrove cut him off once again with, "Captain, please, if I may? Charlie, I'm sure you understand, that philosophically speaking there's really nothing you *have* to do in life if you don't want to. But realistically, each of us make choices every day. You made a conscious choice to become a US Naval officer, and you took an oath to live up to what that means. I'm going to call this a 'request' to help us do our part in trying to save as many American and Vietnamese lives as we can in what's left of this war. If you don't agree to help, well, that's your choice, but I'm sure you know there will be repercussions."

Charlie was now speaking mostly to the commander and said, "Of course, I will help you. I know I took an oath, and I'll not go back on it, it's just that it puts me in a terrible position, especially as an advisor. I spent the last three months building trust with Dao and the team here at the shipyard and with the Vietnamese family from the racetrack. If they get a hint that I'm a spy, I'll lose all credibility and effectiveness."

Commander Hargrove responded by saying, "I completely understand this and want you to maintain your current responsibilities and work and social routines. It's just that we want a set of eyeballs out there and within the community of these individuals and if you notice anything that you feel is suspicious you contact my office."

The rest of the meeting wound down to minor details and Charlie didn't remember anything after that. His mind was working on how this would change things with Kim.

As they streamed out of the office, Margot slipped a little glance that met Charlie's eyes that said, *I feel your pain, man.* They turned a corner out of sight and Charlie whispered under his breath, "I need a drink, I'm going to take a walk."

Margot winked okay at him.

Chapter Eleven

Meeting in the Basilica

Charlie went back to his desk, locked it, then returned to see Margot and said, "Joe and Danh are in Mi Tho working on a rocket screen for the boat pier. I'm going to lunch and probably won't be back today. See you tomorrow."

Margot gestured to a small folder on her desk. "Commander Hargrove left his contact information. I'll keep it for you till tomorrow."

"Thanks, Margot."

Charlie needed to get away from that environment and think. He walked out of the shipyard gate and headed down Ben Bach Dang Street toward the City Wharf where the downtown streets ended at the Saigon River. The sun was shining, and the air felt cool and dry against a china blue sky. He needed to rethink the last day and a half. Maybe he would talk things over with Margot after work. He trusted her as a normal level-headed person. Sometimes, it seemed, one of the few.

Fishing junks motored by, back from early morning fishing grounds near the South China Sea only fifteen miles away. A medium-weight freighter gave two blasts of the ship's horn as it maneuvered passed the wharf, heading for the commercial port at Newport. He stood and looked out as far as he could see to the east side of the Quay.

Charlie went over the morning meeting in his mind and concluded: *I need to settle down. Why am I so riled? I'll think the situation through. It may not be all that bad. After all, I don't have any real intelligence on Bao and may never be in a position to have any. They didn't ask me to go looking for trouble, so I'll follow orders and not.* It puzzled him that neither the captain nor anyone else seemed to care about the episode near An Loc. He expected to be pumped for information regarding the NVA forces. So why get riled?

He walked over to the edge of the wharf and leaned on the wrought iron railing. The sea birds dived and hung in the breeze, waiting for a handout from him. They got none so they moved on. He breathed in the warm trade wind air that seemed to reach as far as the South China Sea. He began to feel better and more settled. He turned north and walked across the large arced plaza and began to stroll up wide Nguyen Hue Boulevard. It was often called the Street of Flowers because of the glorious display of flowers in the stalls during the New Year Holiday.

On up the boulevard he passed the USO on his left and for a moment considered calling his sister, Brigitte, now a junior at Ohio State in Columbus. The USO was the best place to call the States. It wasn't cheap, though, at $3 a minute. No cell phones, no email in those days ... only letter writing or the *occasional* phone call. Because of the cost, most GIs avoided the phones except for emergencies. Those who did call wives or sweethearts regularly rarely indulged more often than every two or three months. Fifty bucks for a fifteen-minute chat started eating into a $400 month's pay.

He checked his watch: nearly noon, a thirteen-hour time difference meant it was 1 a.m. in the dorm. It would take at least thirty minutes to get a line … even college kids don't hang out that late on a weekday. He nixed the idea of calling Brigitte and meandered across Lam Square to the foot of Tu Do (Freedom Street), then headed north.

Tu Do was called Rue Catinet during French Colonial days and was sort of the Fifth Avenue of Saigon. There were many upscale shops, restaurants, and hotels, including the famous Continental Palace on the corner of Le Than Ton Street. The war had forced more bars to open on Tu Do since the Americans had been here. Charlie stopped at a coffeehouse named Café François and ordered an espresso. He sat on the small outdoor patio in front of the shop and leafed through the *Saigon Post*. There were headlines and a story about An Loc. Nothing he didn't know already. An update on Quang Tri explained the fighting was intensifying. It didn't seem interesting anymore; he had played his part yesterday and didn't want to be reminded.

He strolled up the tree-lined street and felt a pang of loneliness. He wished he had called Brigitte. He stopped at Gia Long Street to admire, in the distance, the twin spires of the red-bricked Basilica of Our Lady (Notre Dame). He had been inside the cathedral once for Mass on his first weekend in Vietnam. It made him think of Kim. He remembered how she prayed yesterday in that barn when things seemed desperate. Was she sobbing in that prayer, even though she said she wasn't? So dark in that barn, couldn't see a thing in there. Hard to believe it was only a day ago. A feeling stirred deep inside him that caused a yearning to be with Kim.

Charlie reached the plaza in front of the basilica and stopped to take in the sight of the large century-old structure and the similarity to its model in Paris. He noticed a few slouching beggars on the front steps and saw that several were women suffering from leprosy. By this time, such a sight was not new to him. And he thought it unbelievable that many still suffered and died from the horrible crippling disease while a cure had existed for more than a hundred years. He readied himself to enter by having a few piasters in his hands. Experience had taught him they would invert their conical hats and crowd him for donations. He stepped over several of them, doled his coins, and entered the vestibule.

Just like his first visit, the church lent a comforting familiarity in a country filled with strange places. He liked the pristine light colors and the pure white statue of Our Lady near the altar. On the right-hand wall were many plaques placed by families or perhaps pilgrims. They were inscribed with the French word *Merci* (literally "thank you"). A gratitude for perhaps a prayer answered, good health, or some other good fortune received. Charlie slipped into a pew near the rear and adjacent to the colorful statue of Saint Michael the Archangel. Saint Michael had been his favorite saint since childhood. With his mighty spear in hand and his foot on the neck of the devil, Saint Michael was a boy's idea of a real soldier and adventurer. Charlie recalled and felt good that Kim also had a favorite in Saint Mary Magdalen.

He sat down and tried to relax his mind in the quiet and sacred environment. Not exactly praying but thinking of how or if he should pray after killing another human being. Though his faith had faded some in recent years, he always believed God was on his side. He could always count on God. After killing a man and in such a brutal fashion, he wasn't sure. Fifteen minutes went by, then someone tapped him on

Chapter Eleven

the shoulder. Charlie turned and was shocked. He said, "What in the world are you doing here?!" He spoke only above a whisper.

Kim said, "I'm meeting a friend to catch a ride back home later this afternoon, so I guess I'm killing time … but what about you? I thought you would be tied up with your authorities for a debriefing or something all day about our episode yesterday."

"Sort of like that. I'm decompressing, you might say."

Kim said, "Can we go outside? We can talk better."

He nodded and they started out. Kim pulled him by his arm into an alcove in the rear of the basilica. She faced him and said, "Charlie, I wanted so badly to see you today … "

Charlie took her in his arms and they kissed long and hard. They walked out the front of the church hand-in-hand. Charlie fumbled with some piaster notes for the lepers, and they walked toward Tu Do Street.

They talked as they strolled. "So you were really killing time … in church?"

"Yes, I stopped in to say a prayer and light a candle for Bao."

"What's wrong with Bao?"

"Nothing, yet. You know, he's meeting with his 'intellectual and political buddies' more and more. My parents are worried he will become involved in something against the government. He really just wishes he could be in University. He has an academic mind. He's just curious, and likes to debate politics. I tell them not to worry, he's just stretching his mind. He's harmless."

"Did you get to light the candle?"

"Oh, yes, I came in before you. I confess I lit a candle and kneeled down and then saw you come in. I was so surprised, and my heart was beating so fast I had to wait a few minutes before I could talk normally." Mutual laughter.

Charlie said, "I'm starving, have you had lunch? I'll buy."

"I'm hungry and will accept your offer. I know a quick place to eat and talk if you're willing to take a chance on me."

"Willing and eager!"

They walked a block over to Hai Ba Trung Street hand-in-hand, then Charlie turned to her and said, "You've really made my day. Everything looks brighter!"

The two of them walked up past the Chinese Embassy and down a small alley into a tiny restaurant in the Triumph Hotel. When they entered the alley, they were out of sight for a few seconds, and he pulled her to him and they kissed again. Kim said, "I'm so glad I'm here with you today. It's wonderful to be together on our own in the city."

At the restaurant she said, "I hope you like this place, not very fancy but delicious food and it's fast! If you trust me I'll order." Gesturing, she pointed on the menu: *American Lunch Special.*

"After yesterday, I think we're good on the trust issue; order away!" A young girl of no more than twelve, wearing bright flip-flops that slid on the tiled floor, brought their order, which was lemon grass soup and ham and cheese on a French bread roll. A tall glass of iced tea was a welcome addition. A Vietnamese pop song was playing and echoed against the tiled floor and bare walls painted a modern light green glade color. Sung by a currently popular girl singer, a favorite of Kim's, the music sounded so typically Vietnamese that it made the atmosphere particularly delightful. They ate and both were eager to talk.

Kim said, "I came in with my father this morning to help him with the horses."

"What happened to the horses anyway, where are they?"

"They're at the track. Their owner is renting space temporarily. He can't go back to their farm. The North Vietnamese Army has taken over the area around An Loc now. I heard the US Military is going to use airpower to support the ARVN. There will probably be a lot of destruction around there. They say so far the NVA is contained, but who knows." Pause. "My father will probably buy both horses. The owner has no place for them now, so he'll need to sell quickly."

Charlie said, "They're good horses, the black reminds me of the horse I had when I was a kid. Mine did not have the breeding like these, but he was fast and big. He was a good one. I called him Black Martin. He was a real slick black, just like the one last night."

"Seems like an unusual name, Charlie."

"Marty or Martin was a name my mother called me sometimes when I was a boy. She liked the name. She told me it was my real father's middle name. We didn't have much information on my real father, his records were lost after WWII. His name was shown as Xavier Duvall on the only document we had, but my mother said that his full name was Xavier Martin Duvall. She penciled it in on the original document. She was still alive when we got the colt. He was real black so we called him Black Martin. She died from polio soon after that. I was about ten then. Most people called me Charlie after that, except my stepfather sometimes called me Marty. After she died, I guess the Marty name gradually went away."

Kim said, "I have an hour before my friend Camille picks me up to go back home. Let's walk a little, I'll give you a tour."

"Wonderful!"

When it was time for Kim to catch her ride back, Charlie said with a big grin, "I heard a rumor that we have a dinner date Wednesday night."

"Oh, I heard that rumor, too," Kim said chuckling, and added, "Dao's wife Phuong said it was a set-up."

"That's okay, I don't mind set-ups!"

"Me neither!" she laughed.

"See you then."

※ ※ ※

When Charlie left Kim it was still early, so he decided to return to the office and see if Danh and I were back from Mi Tho. He reached the office around 3 p.m., and we had just walked in. Danh was leaving to pick up his kids. Charlie wanted to talk about the morning meeting he'd had with the captain and Hargrove and asked if I wanted to grab a beer at Kenny's American. "Let's go," I said. I was parched. We hailed a taxi and were there in ten minutes. We started with a couple of PBRs, not the best, but the most popular beer in Vietnam (Pabst Blue Ribbon for the uninitiated). Charlie asked what my security clearance was. I told him SECRET.

"Good," he said. "I want your take on what came out of the meeting this morning. The meeting was designated SECRET. The only people in the meeting were me, Hargrove, Margot, and the captain. You gotta keep this between you and me, old buddy."

"Buckeyes honor."

"You dog." Pause for chuckles and swigs. "Okay, it was a wild meeting. The captain got mad, I got mad. Commander Hargrove tried to keep cool. I was steamed after the meeting, but I've cooled off now after thinking it over. My expectation going in was the meeting would be a debriefing of my run-in with the NVA yesterday. I even made notes of what I thought could be valuable military information. Like the tanks I saw and where they were digging in when we left. That wasn't what the captain wanted at all. He had a Navy Intelligence officer there, Commander Hargrove. The only thing the captain cared about was the fact that I spent all day with Kim, and that I was good friends with the Binh family. They basically want me to spy on Kim's brother, Bao. According to the commander, they have information that he's been meeting with a known Viet Cong operative.

"Hmm. Did he use the word *spy*?"

"No, not the exact word. And, looking back, I must say Hargrove seemed like a reasonable guy. In fact, if he hadn't been there, things could have gotten out of control. Eagleton said some pretty nasty and racist things for a senior Navy officer."

"What was Margot's reaction?" I asked.

"Margot was pretty cool, trying not to take sides, and she shot me a look of sympathy when we walked out. The meeting was probably a valuable slice of learning in her quest to be part of the diplomatic corps."

"Maybe it wasn't as bad as it sounded at first," I told him. "Maybe it was just Eagleton being Eagleton, you got riled, and the commander kept the peace. Is that about it?"

Charlie first thought that was too simple a summary, then said, "You're probably right as usual. You know I took a long walk this afternoon. When I came out of there I was pissed. But I got to thinking, Hargrove said just keep doing what I'm doing, and only if I see anything suspicious to report to him."

"Exactly, that would have been my take, don't borrow trouble. If you don't notice anything suspicious, it'll probably blow over after a few weeks anyway."

"Another beer?"

"Yeah, and see if Kenny has any of those pretzel thingies."

Chapter Twelve

Waterfront Walk

Dusk had wandered into darkness along the Old City Wharf on the Saigon River. A warm light breeze teased the tassels that hung from the screens high overhead the wide and curving river walkway. Two couples strolled slowly beneath the lanterns that gleamed on the water which moved slowly toward the South China Sea. The moon was low and not yet above the tall palms cutting a clean silhouette on the opposite side of the wide river. Little lanterns flickered on the small sampans passing downstream that carried families home at close of day. Only the rocket screens above the restaurants and bars hinted that this was anything but a peaceful exotic paradise.

 The couples were seated by the friendly maître d' of the Piccolo Restaurant. Their table by a window had a perfect view of the river. All spirits were high as the group of four interacted well together. They enjoyed a meal of Vietnamese delicacies recommended by Dao and Phuong, and conversation was light and cheerful. A highlight was Dao's explanation and enthusiasm of the projects he and Charlie were pursuing to help the defense of Quang Tri. Dao's excitement and interest was contagious and all lauded him for his work. It had the effect of bringing hope and it seemed to spark an unexpected bonding of the little group in their allegiance to South Vietnam. Kim wished her father had been there to recognize how dedicated the younger generation was to winning this war.

After two hours of delightful conversation, Dao and Phuong said their "goodnights" and headed to their VW Bug parked up the street behind the Splendid Hotel. They had a babysitter to get home. It had been a wonderful evening so far. Dao and Phuong were gracious hosts.

Charlie was lucky to have drawn Dao as his counterpart. Some of the other advisor-counterpart teams weren't so lucky. Dao understood Charlie, and vice-versa. Dao had been looking for a way to thank Charlie for "bailing" him out of the police brig in Can An last month, and tonight's dinner at Piccolo's could not have been better.

As Kim and Charlie walked toward downtown, she said, "Wow, I can't believe how much you guys are doing to win this war! I am so proud of you both."

"Actually, I really enjoy my job; we're starting to feel like we're making a difference."

"I'm having a wonderful time tonight, Charlie, let's walk a bit. It's so pleasant out this evening."

"I'm glad Camille is letting you stay at her apartment tonight."

"I know, she's a good friend … and she wants to know so much about you!"

"Me?"

"Sure, like how I met such a handsome American Navy guy! And does he have any friends she can meet? She will probably pester me all night about you. Ha!"

They strolled past the statue of Tran Hung Dao by the waterfront. "My father speaks about Tran Hung Dao with reverence, almost as if he were God himself. He was a great hero of the VN Navy who won great battles."

Charlie said, "I know a little about him from the quick culture course advisors attended to prepare for Vietnam." They strolled on.

Kim said "Know something I've always wanted to do?"

"What?"

"Sit on the verandah of the Continental Palace and have an aperitif! Now that's something I've never done before."

"Me neither. Let's do it," Charlie agreed.

"Maybe we'll see a celebrity there! You know sometimes French actors and celebrities show up."

They walked the two blocks over and climbed the steps. It wasn't busy. Charlie ordered drinks: a champagne cocktail for Kim and French brandy for himself.

They sat and looked down at couples walking hand-in-hand slowly up from the waterfront, passing the sidewalk verandah. They were silent in their thoughts, comfortable with each other. Finally Kim said, "What's it like in America? I've only read about it in books, and seen movies, of course."

"America? It's not that different from right here, right now. Couples coming back from dinner, having an evening talk, relaxing after a long day. If we were sitting on Union Square, San Francisco, in the summer, you could hardly tell the difference. Oh, if you are in the countryside or the farmland, it's a different life than downtown. But you have cities, countryside, rivers and mountains and seashores in Vietnam, like us. The people in America come from everywhere in the world. Some call it a melting pot."

Charlie went on. "One thing I've learned in my limited travels in the US and here is that all-in-all people seem to be about the same. Most have a family, take care of their kids, work hard all day, come home, play with the kids awhile, eat and relax. I believe most people want to do what's right … not all, but most. I guess that's not a very profound statement, is it? What do you believe about people?"

"I believe you're one of those people who want to do the right thing."

"Huh, sometimes I wonder about that." They sipped their drinks, and then the calm was broken by a loud argument across the street between a drunken American civilian and a cyclo-taxi driver. The dispute was settled rather abruptly when the police escorted the man away.

Kim said, "Do you feel okay now about our 'adventure' on Thursday?"

"I feel better. I took a long walk in the afternoon. I'm okay, I guess. It's just that though we trained for it, I never ever thought I would have to kill another person. It makes me feel like somehow I've moved over to the other side of humanity, the ones who are capable of brutality. When he swung that sten at us, I didn't hesitate, I shot that kid without even thinking. I mean he was just a kid, he had his whole life, and he's got parents that probably are at his service right now, for cripes sake."

They were quiet for a while, and then he said, "What about you, Kim?"

"I couldn't sleep Thursday night, I felt badly for that kid too, but we … or rather you had no choice. You did what you had to do; you saved my life, Charlie. I'll never forget that, or ever be able to repay you for that." After a while she went on. "This will get better with time. Sorry to say, I have some experience with this. Unfortunately as the war goes on, trauma has become common. I have friends dealing with war trauma, death and guilt. It does get better with time." She took his hand in both of hers and squeezed it against her cheek. "It just means you have a heart; that's why I like you, Charlie."

Charlie said earnestly, "You know you're the only one I'll ever be able to talk to about this. The way we are talking now, that is. No one will ever understand this the way you and I do."

Then she said in a kind and thoughtful way, "I should tell you, Charlie, my father is so thankful and so proud of you. I heard him tell Mother that Lieutenant Strickland is a very brave but also kind officer, and that we were so lucky that I was with you when the Tigers came. He could hardly speak of it without being emotional. I wasn't supposed to hear. For the first time I saw the years beginning to weigh on him a little."

Charlie said, "He is a good man. I could tell that right away." A little pause, then, "It's getting late, I must get you to your friend's apartment. I'll get a taxi and drop you." Charlie hailed a Blue and White on Tu Do Street. Before they left the Continental, Charlie asked, "Did you see any celebrities?"

"Just one, he was wearing a Navy uniform."

They climbed into the snug rear seat of the Renault, and Charlie said, "134 Nguyen Trai, Cholon, please." The small man at the wheel nodded.

Kim turned to Charlie and said, "What a great time I had with you tonight. I feel comfortable and happy when I'm with you." He pulled her close; she put her arms around him and they kissed long and passionately until the driver stopped and said, "Monsieur, 134 Nguyen Trai, s'il vous plaît."

Charlie walked her to the apartment. They said goodnight and promised to see each other soon. Then Charlie left in the taxi.

Chapter Thirteen

Life Goes On

Charlie and Dao dived into their projects and worked long hours. They were making great headway with priority on the skimmer, which would be the fastest water vessel in their fleet. The intended use would be for intelligence and communications with larger VN Navy ships capable of fire power in the area around Quang Tri.

They had made two extended full performance range field tests in the waters two miles out from Saigon reserved for the Navy tests. The boat had performed in excellent fashion in speed and handling. But there was a torsional vibration issue in the power train that had shown up at around two-thirds peak design speed which shook the vessel, then disappeared at the very high speeds.

Fortunately, they had a recent university engineering graduate named Tuyen on their VN Navy Engineering team whose specialty was vibration. He was assigned the primary mathematical analysis. But these were the days before many computers, so the calculations were laborious. Charlie had pulled some strings and they were able to acquire two of the latest programmable Texas Instruments hand-held calculators, which speeded things up considerably. Among Charlie, Dao, and the new guy, they were determined to solve the issue. This meant Charlie worked long hours and through the next two weekends.

In the meantime, Kim had been busy at the track sorting out the newly purchased horses. It turned out the gray and the two new ones were the best racehorse potentials they now had. Binh had decided to sell the remaining two in his barn. Kim was busy training and exercising these three while her father was busy contacting potential buyers for the others.

Because of their busy lives, Kim and Charlie had not seen each other for more than two weeks. Charlie was somewhat conflicted about this. He wanted to see her but was trying to avoid being exposed to any unwanted knowledge about Bao. He worried that Eagleton would call him in any day and ask about the "spy work." Life went on in this way.

Chapter Fourteen

Talk with Mother

A week after the evening at the Piccolo, Kim was helping her mother clean up after dinner and asked if she could talk to her in a mother-daughter way. They had an open relationship and trusted each other completely. They would have these talks from time to time. "Of course," she answered in her gentle, smiling way. "Let's go to the garden. It's more private and it's cooler there."

They sat down side-by-side on the small settee with their cups of hot tea. Kim pulled her knees up under her chin and clasped her arms about them. Averting her eyes, she asked Therese, "What do you and Father think of Lieutenant Strickland…Charlie? Do you have any thoughts about him?"

"Oh, Kim, I have been thinking you would be coming to me. I'm not that old that I don't notice things. Of course we have our thoughts of Lieutenant Strickland. They are all positive." Therese held her beautiful smile on her daughter for a few moments and said, "He has made quite an impression on your father. He thinks the world of Lieutenant Strickland. I also think he's a wonderful man. He seems honorable and to have good values."

Kim said, "I wanted to ask your opinion, because…well, I like him a lot and I think he likes me, too. Right now, it's just a good friendship. We have so many things in common, and we spent so much time being so close to each other the day in An Loc that I feel I now know him very well. But I believe…if I let it…our relationship will soon go further than friendship. And," she paused a couple of seconds, "I know things will get very complicated after that."

"Kim, you're my daughter and I can feel your struggle. You are a beautiful young woman, a beautiful person. Charlie sees that, too. And I'm sure he sees the same complications. These are the tough choices that we all must face in life. And they are tougher in a world like ours. He is an American; you are a Vietnamese woman. You both love your countries. These are such uncertain times. We don't know what the future holds for our country. I wouldn't dare say this to your father, but I fear we will not hold our country together without the Americans. And I believe the Americans will certainly be gone within a year. They are leaving so quickly, even I notice it. These are all the things we must consider. That you must consider."

She continued, "And, yes, our family must consider these things also. Your father is on a military disability retirement from the Republic of Vietnam. What happens to that? We don't know what the future holds."

Kim said, "What if he asks me to go to America when he leaves? If he asks me to marry him? This is all hypothetical, of course. He has said nothing about this, but sometimes I wonder if he is thinking about this, like me. How would you and Father feel?"

Chapter Fourteen

"If you love him, Kim, and he loves you, and you leave Vietnam, of course we will be sad and miss you. But we want what's best for you, and trust you to make that decision. Who knows? We may have to leave also. You know your father fought for many years with the ARVN, and a short while with the French. He will likely be considered an enemy of North Vietnam. We may have no choice. We don't know what a new policy may be. Decisions will have to be made as they come before us, Kim."

She put her arm around Kim and looking directly into her eyes said, "We respect you as an intelligent adult woman, Kim, to make your own sometimes difficult life choices as you see fit. That's how we tried to raise you. But always remember: we will always support you in any way we can." She kissed Kim's forehead.

"Thank you, Mother."

Chapter Fifteen

Saigon Zoo

During the next few weeks of April and early May, Charlie and Kim had only a few small chances to meet. The Easter Offensive instigated by North Vietnam was intensifying. The Quang Tri area was becoming a bloody struggle to hold the NVA in check. Charlie and Dao and their team were working "24-7" on their skimmer project to support defensive positions on-shore and off-shore near Quang Tri. They had solved the vibration problem with a novel hydraulic damper developed by the team, and they had sent five skimmer speed boats reworked with the new engine and pump package to a place called Wunder Beach just offshore Quang Tri. So far the VN Navy was pleased with their performance.

In the An Loc area, the NVA units had destroyed the city of Loc Ninh by April 11, and a full-throated attack on the city of An Loc was launched by the NVA on April 12. Units of the NVA and VC had the city under siege shortly thereafter. ARVN had pushed them back and the US Airforce was pounding the enemy with firepower on some of the most open targets the pilots had seen in the war.

In addition to those at Quang Tri and An Loc, the NVA had launched a third invasion on April 12 from Cambodia bases into the Central Highlands of South Vietnam, seeking to capture Kontum. The Easter Offensive had turned into a three-pronged attack. All were in full bloom by the end of April. Charlie and Dao as Navy engineers had no part in the defense of An Loc or Kontum so they poured all their resources, 24-7, into supporting the units at Quang Tri.

While these NVA offenses did not militarily affect most of the large Mekong Delta directly, they caused a great deal of worry about what the future held for people like Binh's family. It was foreboding enough just to think that the NVA could so easily attack and destroy at will from outside the Vietnam border—and so close to their Delta homes and farms.

Kim had been working more at the track with the new horses and had ridden in two special races during a festival that had been delayed earlier. She was excited that she had won a race on the black horse that had carried Charlie to safety. She had hoped Charlie could have been there with her. She wondered if they would drift apart if his intense work schedule lasted into the months. Actually she had no need to worry, for the few times that Charlie and I got out for a beer during this period, Charlie talked of nothing but Kim.

They finally did get together at the beginning of May. They arranged a date on a Saturday afternoon. Kim was sitting at a park bench at the National Zoological Park and Museum. The Zoo Parkland was one of the most beautiful places in the city. The grounds were a botanical garden densely populated with hundreds of Asian species of trees, flowers, and fauna that rose from a manicured grassy setting of hidden pathways leading to dozens of secret lily ponds, and small shallow streams of exotic fish and forbidden rendezvous. Pagodas appeared as though dropped in from above, displaying Asian wildlife and ancient artifacts. The central building was a magnificent pagoda displaying ancient treasures. Overall, the park gave the impression of a large enchanted woods of nature lighted by streams of sunlight.

Charlie was walking quickly with the aid of a park map to meet Kim at the agreed point. Presently he saw her sitting in the distance reading a book and unaware of his approach. He was suddenly taken aback by her beauty and stopped in the pathway. A tender light caught the side of her face in oblique, and a chill ran down his spine as he took in the reality of the moment. The curve of her neck as it met her chin, her lips partially hidden by long black hair that fell across her delicate but irrepressible femininity. The way her small hands held her book. The tilt of her head as she read her book. *Who am I to be so lucky as to be loved by such a person? A person in possession of such beauty, intellect, and character. And who am I to be the one that such a person waits for on a park bench, rejecting all others? Only a few weeks ago I didn't even know a soul like this existed.*

Charlie suddenly knew he wanted never to be away from her. He knew he loved her and always would. He slowed his walk and passed into a cool dark glade as he approached her. Kim saw him and put the book down. She arose, her cheeks flushed with the rose of excitement, and rushed to meet him. Her feet light upon the mossy earth and her heart filled with anticipation. They embraced with a joy of youth and love and longing fulfilled that few in this world are ever lucky enough to know.

"Charlie, my darling, I missed you so much, and I love you so." She whispered her secret to the cool dark glade. He pressed her small feminine body so close against his that he felt each beat of her heart.

"And I love you, Kim. We'll make this work someway."

Chapter Sixteen

Call in the Night

On the evening of May 10, Charlie was stretched out on his cot reading a bit before turning in. *Pitcairn's Island* was the book, the third in the *Bounty Trilogy* by Nordhoff and Hall. He was absorbed in this book of the South Seas. He was starting to think he didn't have it so bad over here after all, at least compared to Fletcher Christian. At 9:30 p.m. the phone rang. "What? Was that my phone?" he mumbled out loud. "My phone never rings; who the devil could be calling me?"

He answered in a quandary, "Hello, Lieutenant Strickland."

"Tiger Central, Lieutenant Strickland please?" Charlie thought, *Hey, that's Squeaky's voice! Ha! I've never actually talked to her.* Squeaky was an operator for the Central Telephone Exchange in South Vietnam. Sometimes the Exchange worked, sometimes it didn't. Squeaky's voice was the GIs most recognized female voice in Vietnam. It was said

GIs would actually call Tiger Central Exchange from the States after their tour was complete just to hear her voice.

"Yes, this is Lieutenant Strickland."

"Hold please, Lieutenant." Short delay with static.

"Hello, Lieutenant, this is Mr. Mi."

"Who?"

"Mi."

"I'm sorry you must be trying to reach … "

"No … you are Charlie, right?"

"Yes, this is Charlie; do I know you?"

"Yes, this is Mr. Mi, from Can An. Remember we met during the police chief incident over there."

The cobwebs cleared a little.

"Okay, I remember now. How can I help you, Mi?"

"It's rather urgent, Lieutenant."

"Urgent, you say. You're coming in very faint, Mi," Charlie said as he raised his voice. "How urgent? It's getting rather late in the day for something urgent."

"It's very urgent, we need to speak tonight privately. You will probably want to take some action on the information I give you. It won't matter tomorrow, it will be too late."

"Well … can you just tell me now?"

"Oh, no, this exchange is not secure. We should meet in private in a secure location. We should meet within the hour. You will want to have time before it gets too late tonight to talk to your people about this matter."

"My people? What people? What's this all about, Mi?"

Mi continued, "I'll explain when we meet; you must hurry. We can meet at the old City Cargo Wharf. Not the wharf at Newport but the downtown wharf. Go to the warehouses. There is plenty of

Chapter Sixteen

light down there tonight, don't worry about trouble. At the rear of the first warehouse you'll see some gambling and betting going on. There is a pit there with several men betting on cockfighting. Just walk past them and enter the warehouse through the tall open door. Walk through the area."

Charlie broke in, "Wait a minute, Mi. Isn't that an opium area? Isn't that where the opium dens are?"

"That's right. Don't worry, they won't care. They won't bother you. Walk right through that area until you see me. It's a little bit dark in the area, but it's private and you'll be able to see me there. I'll be alone. But there's no time to waste."

Charlie said, "Sounds ominous."

"Yes, I understand that, but you need to know this. How long will it take you to get here?"

Charlie said, "You're asking me to take quite a leap of faith here, Mi. I mean, an opium den in the dark? Can't you tell me more? Does it concern Binh's family?"

Silence for ten seconds, then, "Yes, indirectly it could."

"All right. Perhaps twenty minutes."

Charlie threw on his Seabee fatigues, grabbed his wallet, and was off. He'd thought of talking to me first, I later learned. But he didn't want to deal with having to share any message if it wasn't shareable. He just left me a quick note for emergency purposes, noting the time he left and where he was headed.

He reached the warehouse in ten minutes, then found the pit with some rough looking characters and a couple of sorry looking black roosters. One old man nodded to Charlie and gestured the way through the opium den. Though the place had little light, Charlie recognized Mi standing by the door at the opposite end of the warehouse.

After Charlie saw Mi, he remembered him better and recalled that he'd had a good impression of Mi when they met in Can An. He remembered a no-nonsense person, though diminutive in appearance. Yes, certainly slight of stature, even for a Vietnamese gentleman, but there was an overall aura about him that made you think confidence and that this was someone who should be listened to. He stood slouched against a cabinet which contained opium paraphernalia. He was dressed in a dark suit jacket and a wide brimmed evening hat and holding a smoking cigarette in a palm-up position, the way they did in Vietnam. Sometimes I thought Mi was too young to have that look naturally. Was that look just a little bit put on? The scene reminded Charlie of a 1940s Hitchcock movie.

Mi quietly nodded a greeting to Charlie, then inhaled a deep drag from his American cigarette. The cigarette glow lighted the exhaled smoke which mixed with the opium air and produced a foul odor. Mi came close to Charlie. "Were you followed, Lieutenant?" he whispered without smiling.

Backing away, Charlie said, "Don't think so, but I wasn't checking for that. Should I have been?"

"Not necessarily, just being cautious. Follow me." They exited a side door and walked quickly through a dark area of industrial workshops. Mi pulled a key from his pocket and unlocked an office door to a machine shop. Charlie followed him in. Mi flipped on a small desk lamp and said, "Please sit down, Lieutenant." After both were settled he said, "Don't be alarmed with all the secrecy, but I mustn't let anyone know I'm meeting with you tonight. You see, we must address a matter of life and death tonight involving a bomb attack."

"Bomb attack?!"

"Let me explain. I'm sure you know that Bao and I are good friends. You may also know that we are members of a political club started at the

University. We meet from time to time to discuss history and politics of Vietnam. We are both interested in politics and hope someday that all of Vietnam will be reunited."

Charlie interrupted, "I'm not sure I like where this is going."

"Please hear me out, Lieutenant."

"Go ahead."

"Bao and I as well, as most of the members of this club at the University, believe the only way to achieve the goal of reunification of Vietnam is through peaceful means of negotiation based on common Vietnamese history, religion, and nationalistic ideals. We believe the two Vietnams have more in common than we have in differences."

"I understand."

Mi went on, "But a small group of three or four individuals have broken from our club and are not willing to give peace a chance. They're impatient for action now. They believe violence is necessary and plan to launch terrorist attacks in the cities to complement the Easter Offensive. I am sorry to tell you there is a plan to detonate a large bomb in downtown Saigon in the early morning hours unless you and I can stop it. I have unwittingly received very reliable information that they plan to blow up the Splendid Hotel BOQ after midnight tonight at 12:30 a.m. I'm sure you know that there are at least forty American officers and men, plus at least six Vietnamese BOQ staff living there. Most will be killed or seriously wounded if this plan is executed."

"Good Lord Almighty! That's only two hours from now."

"To put it bluntly, I am not in favor of the American military being here in our country, but I cannot agree to this type of killing. The Americans are standing down now, anyway, and in less than a year they, *you*, will be gone. I'm asking you to make some calls to head this off."

Charlie said, "You can call the Saigon police branch and alert them to intercede, no?"

"Perhaps, but I doubt if they would listen. First, there are many calls of this nature that come in. Most are false alarms. The capital police wouldn't believe me unless I disclosed my identity and how I acquired the information, and maybe not even then. They wouldn't have time to investigate the information before they would have needed to act. And second, in my opinion, the Americans are more efficient and have more of an incentive to act quickly with the number of Americans at risk. Also, the Saigon police would likely respond immediately if the request came from the American authorities."

Mi stopped talking to let the information sink in.

Charlie said, "Just place a call from a call box downtown, you'll be anonymous. They'll surely at least check it out."

"Lieutenant, I'm telling you there's not enough time. If we had twenty-four hours, maybe, but they just don't move on a tip that quickly. Too many false alarms. It would not be a priority."

Charlie sat and thought, and Mi started again. "I understand you have a contact in the NIS, a Commander Hargrove?"

Charlie exploded. "Now how in the hell would you know that?!"

"Please, we just cannot afford to get excited," Mi said, then calmly, "Lieutenant, there are many channels of communication in Saigon. Some are official, some are secret, and some are practically mystic. This city has been known for intrigue for centuries. It would serve no purpose tonight to discuss all the how's and why's information is passed in this city. It's my belief that no one knows that I possess this information about an attack—except for you, of course. I came upon it quite by accident. I also happen to know that you have been "asked" to keep an eye out especially regarding Bao, Kim's brother. I'm not at liberty to tell you how I know that. I believe if you contacted Hargrove stating someone had passed an anonymous note or message or call to you, it would be sufficient to trigger Hargrove and stop a slaughter. I would ask that you keep our names, mine and Bao's, confidential. I am sure that Bao had *nothing* to do with this, and I *know* I had nothing to do with it."

"Frankly, Mi, I think it sounds risky for *you*. Are you not concerned that one or more of the perpetrators could be arrested? Under the pressure of torture they would likely provide names of the members of your whole political club and perhaps cause you and/or Bao to be arrested?"

Mi responded coolly with, "Not in the least. Even if one or more of the perpetrators are arrested and gives the names of those in the club, neither Bao nor I are connected in any way to a bomb. We would have alibis because we have nothing to do with this bomb. Also, my belief is you, Lieutenant, would have incentive to keep our names out."

"Well! What a situation! You leave me with no viable alternatives. I'm going back to my quarters to have a think before I do anything."

Mi started, "You must promise me … "

"I'll promise you nothing. I said I'd think it over. I'll tell you this much: I'll not disclose you as a source unless I'm forced to by the US Navy. Now, how can I contact you if necessary?"

Mi handed him a small card and said, "Here's a number of a person who can reach me quickly. I'm usually at the University library on weekdays in the afternoon. I have a part-time job there."

Mi said, "We must part now, Lieutenant. I'm sure you will do what's right. I'll leave first. Wait five minutes before you leave. It's best to take a different route in return."

Charlie took a circuitous route back to the shipyard. By the time he returned he had decided to contact Hargrove. He had an inclination to trust Commander Hargrove and figured being straight with him was the safest thing to do for all concerned. He would tell the whole story and emphasize he could not disclose the name of his informant. He pulled out the contact information that Margot had given him and called the NIS Commander immediately. It was 10:45 p.m. Within ten minutes, the call went through and Hargrove was on the line.

"Yes, Charlie, what is it?"

Charlie immediately knew he had made the right decision. He heard a friendly voice and felt the tremendous strength of the US Navy at the other end of the telephone line.

"Commander, I've just had a discussion with a person that informed me of a major life-and-death event planned within hours. Time is of the greatest urgency; we need to speak."

"Do we have twenty minutes to talk?"

"Yes, sir."

"Do you know the informant?"

"Yes, sir."

"Do you trust the informant?"

"Yes, sir."

"Are you at your billet at the shipyard?"

"Yes, sir."

"I'll meet you outside your billet in ten minutes. I'll be in a black Navy sedan. Stay in your BOQ till I get there. Talk to no one. See you in ten minutes."

"Very good, sir."

Chapter Seventeen

The Bomb

Commander Hargrove showed up outside Charlie's BOQ at the shipyard on schedule as promised: in ten minutes. Two heavy duty shore patrol were in the front seat. Hargrove was in the back seat. Charlie watched the black sedan pull up slowly to the front entrance. It made Charlie think: *Where in the hell did they come from? To get organized, get a car, furnish it with a front seat full of 450 pounds of Navy beef including weapons and gear and get over here in ten minutes! Amazing!*

The rear door in front of Charlie swung open and the friendly face of Hargrove said, "Hop in, Lieutenant." Hargrove told the driver to pull over to a small parking lot at the side of the BOQ. "Okay, Charlie, tell me what you know. Don't worry, we're all family in here, at or above SECRET."

Charlie told him everything that happened since he'd received Mi's call. Then he said, "The informant requested anonymity, and I told him I would do what I could to respect his request."

Commander Hargrove said, "I don't want to know the identity of your informant. After all, he wouldn't be much of an informant if we exposed him. Maybe he'll be useful in the future. My recommendation would be to stay on good terms with him."

"What's next, Commander?"

"We'll go over to the Splendid, take a look-see first. It's after 11 p.m. now. We'll clear the place by 11:30, then send in the UDT Team (bomb squad) and the dogs to try to locate explosives."

"Need anything from me?"

"Nope, you're done for the night. Go to bed. And please don't show up at the Splendid Hotel tonight. You definitely don't want to be seen there. Thanks for your help."

Charlie opened the car door and jumped out. The black sedan pulled out of the Navy shipyard. Charlie slowly went back to his billet relieved but also a little deflated that he wasn't asked to go with them. He picked up *Pitcairn's Island* and stretched out again to read. He couldn't concentrate, though; his mind was too wound up and he lay there going over the happenings of the evening. As he tried to recall each detail he felt better and better that he had done the right thing. Then he became drowsy and drifted off, dreaming of boyhood days with his stepfather.

In the dream, Charlie and his stepfather were riding their horses along the cattle lane. He was talking about being a farmer and horseman when he grew up. He was trying to please his father, telling him he, too, wanted to be a farmer. He would have horses and a farm of his own that his father could come and visit. But there was something wrong. Maybe his father wouldn't be alive when he got his farm. Maybe he would be far away and couldn't get back to be with his father. Maybe something else was drawing him away that he favored, but was

Chapter Seventeen

afraid if he told his father it would be hurtful to him. His father was trying to call him to let him know it was okay. But Charlie could not hear him and could not get to the phone, which was ringing, and it rang and rang.

Suddenly he woke up and realized his phone was ringing. He glanced at his watch. It was nearly 1:30 a.m.

"Hello, this is Lieutenant Strickland."

"Charlie, this is Hargrove."

"Yes, sir, Commander."

"Well, it looks like we're wrapped up over here tonight. We cleared the place and the UDT boys and their dog found the bomb, a pretty hefty bomb. Would have done some real damage. But no damage, no one hurt. All the occupants have gone back into the building. Made one arrest, but of course he's not talking. For your information, it's not the person we spoke of before. And I'm sure your informant would not be that stupid to be there."

Charlie said, "That's the best outcome we could have hoped for."

"You bet, Charlie, and you are to thank. You made a good decision to alert us. I'll take care of summarizing for the captain. You don't need to get involved. I understand the situation with the captain. Get some rest."

"Goodnight, sir."

Charlie lay back down on his cot, now relaxed. He thought about Kim and felt a desire to share the good news with her. But he knew that would never be possible. After all, he was a spy.

Funny thing about people, Charlie and I often said. A good person in civilian life is probably going to make a good Naval Officer: trustworthy, kind, smart, brave and comfortable in their own skin seemed to be what you want. You follow those kind of people, civilian *or* military.

You want to work hard for them and do your best for them. We found out weeks after this incident that Navy Intelligence Officer Hargrove had grabbed a flak jacket, helmet, borrowed a face mask and went into that Hotel with the UDT team that night. Hargrove had all those good qualities. Braver than most. We agreed he was probably the finest Naval officer we knew during our stint in the Navy.

Chapter Eighteen

Country Girl

Five months had passed in Vietnam. We had made it to June and nearly half of our tour was over. We were getting on well with our counterparts. I was doing lots of travelling around the Delta with Danh, and we'd completed housing and electrification projects on several of the small bases on the rivers. We'd just returned from building a community center in the small settlement of Nam Can on the southern edge of the Cau Mau Peninsula. Charlie and Dao had received an award for their work on two patrol boat models upgraded with technical improvements in speed and armaments. Charlie and Kim were getting thicker and thicker. And best of all, it had been a month since the bomb threat had been foiled, and no repercussions. Things in general were going good, I'd say.

After six months in-country, US personnel were entitled to a two-week vacation, referred to as R&R. A week into June, Charlie and I were in the process of deciding where we would go for our break. I was thinking Australia; Charlie was thinking of going to see his sister, Brigitte. He wanted to explain to her the situation with Kim: that he was thinking of marriage and bringing Kim to the US. Brigitte was the only family he had, except for an elderly aunt who was Brigitte's guardian and with whom Brigitte was living while in college. Charlie felt strongly about family and wanted Brigitte to be assured that Kim would never come between him and Brigitte.

Yes, all in all, things seemed under control ... until they weren't. That's when Country Girl showed up. It was Friday, June 9. Bao was at his meeting with his political club at the University. As they were about to start, a diminutive girl carrying a book bag came into the room. A very pretty girl who appeared to be about eighteen or nineteen with big dark eyes and an engaging smile. Bao later described her as a girl from the countryside because of the simple shift dress she wore; a "country girl."

She introduced herself as Tam and informed the others at the meeting that she would be joining them for the rest of the semester. It was an assignment her professor had given her to broaden her knowledge in current events in the political science class she was taking at the University. She hoped it would be okay with everyone. The club, made up of young males, said it was definitely okay.

The thing is, just before she sat down she turned and glanced straight at Bao with those big dark and dusky eyes, just long enough to connect eyeball to eyeball with a soft little smile intended for him only. Now if Mi had been there that late afternoon, which he wasn't, and being more worldly than Bao, he would have recognized that smile as an "experienced smile"—and maybe a red flag.

During the discussions, some members made comments on the proposal Bao had made the prior meeting for a type of democracy that would work for a unified Vietnam. Tam asked the question: What is the real reason behind the VC terrorizing the countryside? Shouldn't the government ask that question instead of spending all their efforts on torturing and killing the VC? Bao thought those were good questions. She's pretty, friendly and smart, too.

Even though Mi wasn't there that afternoon, it was clear to Bao that there was something different about Tam. She was more than smart, she was highly intelligent. He sensed that she could handle herself in many situations. He believed her more complex than first appeared. There was something about Country Girl that was attractive to Bao.

After the meeting, he mustered the courage to introduce himself and bought her a French le crème glacée at the little snack shop in the University building. They talked a bit. She said she was from south of Mi Tho, a small village in the Delta, and some community people were sponsoring her at the University. Then she said she must excuse herself, for she had to care for her two young siblings.

Bao said, "See you next time."

"I hope so, it was nice," she said.

She walked away quickly down the street as a white Mazda four-door pulled out of street parking. She turned the corner and after she was out of sight of the University, the Mazda sped up to her and the Country Girl quickly jumped into the front passenger seat. The car motored over to Plantation Road, then turned right and drove a mile on Plantation Road, passing by the racetrack, then made another turn into a slum area. They crossed a marginal looking one-lane bridge and continued slowly a short distance on the narrow unpaved street and stopped.

Tam got out in front of a fragile-looking hovel of corrugated sheet metal and plywood with a fiberglass roof. It was wedged in between two similar structures with just enough room to walk between. She had one hour before the car would return and take her for her evening work. In that time she must care for her mother and prepare her for the night. She must also prepare food and feed her mother and the two little ones before she readied herself. She would not eat herself, for she knew Madame Jeanette would have a little something for her when she got to the Palace.

She whispered a silent prayer: "Thank you, Jesus, for the ice cream at 4:30 from that nice kid." She walked in and went straight to her bedridden mother. "Mother, are you all right?"

"Yes, okay, just need the toilette." Tam brought the vessel and then prepared the small amount of rice and soup she had secured early that morning at Catholic Charities on Hong Tap Tu Street. There was half a baguette which she would divide into three. Within ten minutes the gas heater on the kitchen floor had dinner heating up.

A plastic basin with a little water provided enough to scrub the faces and hands of the four- and five-year-old. She dried them off and sat them down to practice counting their numbers and to read them a story in their comic book. They sat on her lap and held Tam tightly against their little bodies. From her book bag she pulled two juice boxes and gave them each one. They smiled at her and said they loved her. Tam told them to eat their suppers while it was hot. While they ate they talked like little twittering birds.

"How was your day, Mother?"

"A good day, we told stories, and then the little ones played outside for a while with Mrs. Tuyen. I'm so grateful we have her. She brought me a *People* magazine. Can you believe it? We talked for a long time this afternoon while the kids slept."

Tam brought the basin with water and sponged her mother and dressed her in a clean gown, then brought her food.

Chapter Eighteen

"How was *your* day, Tami?"

"I had a good day, too. I met a nice boy at the University. Very polite. I'm beginning to look forward to some more money I will be getting from my job. I believe soon we will have enough money to get an apartment in the city. And you will be more comfortable. We will have regular reliable water. I feel so much better today. The people in my discussion group were very interesting and the boy was so nice. It really lifted my spirits, and maybe I will see him again at school."

"Hurry and get ready for your job, Tami, or you will be late." Tam pulled a curtain across the room, removed her clothing, and gave herself a sponge bath with the rest of the dirty water. Then changed into a sequined miniskirt and a black dressy top. She saved the eye makeup and cheap perfume to apply at the Palace, so as not to disgrace her mother.

She kissed the young siblings and her mother good night as the white Mazda pulled up. It was dusk now and she was looking at six hours of pain and disgrace. But she was resolute and said to herself, *I will get through this.*

Tam's handler pulled the white Mazda up in front of the Emperor's Palace Bar on Tu Do Street. Before she got out he spoke to Tam earnestly. "Okay, I'll pick you up at 12 midnight sharp. Remember your name, right?"

"Yeah, sure: Suzie."

"Also remember at all times, the money is important but not as important as *secrets*. Listen for *military secrets*, it's important for the cause."

"You don't need to remind me of the cause," Tam told him. "If I didn't believe in the cause, I wouldn't be here."

"Okay, good, remember: Americans have big loud voices. The higher the rank, usually the better the secrets. The better you do, the more money you get. Good luck."

Tam glared at him, but said nothing. As she opened the car door, she changed mentally from country girl Tam into bar girl Suzie. She walked straight into the bar and smiled at a couple of GIs as she entered. One of them shouted, "Hey, what's your name, Miss?" She sang back, "My name Suzie, handsome!" Then walked straight through the bar and found Madame Jeanette.

"Hello, Suzie. Hey, there's some food here I saved, some good pizza, if you're hungry."

"Thanks, I'm starved." In fact, she was faint with hunger; she'd had only the small ice cream since 7 a.m. She ate quickly, put on her makeup and went straight to work in the front bar with her goal to obtain *enemy military secrets* and *money,* in that order.

Chapter Nineteen

Emperor's Palace

Charlie and Margot were walking past the American Embassy a few minutes after they left their office in the shipyard. It was Friday afternoon, June 9, at 6 p.m. and Margot was cashing in her rain check for the pizza Charlie had promised. It was supposed to be a threesome, but I was busy helping Danh unload some building material he'd bought for a project at his house. "So where's the best pizza in Saigon, Ms. Ambassador?"

"Well, I heard the Emperor's Palace has genuine imitation Italian pizza."

Charlie said, "Okay, then, the Emperor's Palace it is. I think that's over on Tu Do. I've never been there myself, but I think if we go two more blocks on Thong Nhat Street, then hang a left we should run into it, if we keep a lookout."

"Great, I've got a taste for pizza tonight. Haven't had pizza since I've been in Vietnam … don't worry, not expecting Pizza Hut."

"Good."

It was only a fifteen minute walk from the Embassy to the "Palace," as the GIs called it. At 6:15 p.m. there was no line yet. They walked straight in and were met by a young, pretty, smiling hostess, "Good evening, my name Jade. You want menu for dinner with the lady, Lieutenant?"

"Yes, menu please."

"Ah, certainly, you take table here. Waitress coming over soon, enjoy."

They were seated at a tall table for two, with barstools. It was a popular Friday night hang-out, not a dive, about half-filled with GIs, a few Army officers and a couple of expats. Lots of chatter, pop music, cigarette and cigar smoke—and many young bargirls working the crowd. A slight girl in six-inch heels that brought her to only five feet tall came from behind the long bar in the back of the room and asked for their drink order. Charlie and Margot decided on 33 Export beer. They also ordered a large Margherita pizza while the waitress/bargirl was there. The same waitress came right back with two beers. Charlie put a two hundred-piaster tip on the table.

"Thank you, sir."

Margot raised her eyebrows and looked at him unapprovingly.

"What? I felt sorry for her. She's not even sixteen."

Margot shrugged. "Charlie Strickland saving the world, one bargirl at a time."

He chuckled.

They were both parched. They clicked "Cheers" and took a long drink, and Charlie drained half his bottle.

"Decide where you're going on R&R?" Margot asked.

"Yeah, I think to see my sister, Brigitte. Maybe I'll even meet her in Hawaii. Now that would be a real vacation. I think she would

Chapter Nineteen

really enjoy that." Charlie thought for a second. "My sis, a good kid. She's my only relative, except for an older aunt. Brigitte has special needs, you know. She's in college, and she has some time in July that would work."

He finished his beer. Margot said she was going to the lady's room. Charlie warned her, "The restroom is probably a little rough."

"I'm not expecting much. Don't worry unless I'm not back in an hour!"

Another bargirl came to their table. A little more glamorous, wearing a gold lamé minidress. "You need another beer, handsome?"

"Yes, please."

"You girlfriend go home?"

"Oh, she's not my girlfriend, just a friend, a colleague. And she's just in the lady's room."

A few minutes later, Miss Gold Lamé came back with his beer. "You need girlfriend tonight, maybe?" she asked.

Charlie said, "Oh, no thanks, I already have a girlfriend." This time he noticed she was older than most of the other bargirls and thought: *I probably should be putting down some tip for each bargirl.*

She said, "Okay, I bring you pizza soon." He put down a hundred-piaster note tip on the table for her.

She said, "Thank you, you kind gentleman."

Margot returned to the table and said, "Well, that was fun!"

"I warned you; but thanks for coming back. The barmaid thinks I need a girlfriend tonight. I was running out of excuses."

"I'll pretend I'm your girlfriend."

"You don't have to; she thinks that already."

The pizza arrived, brought by Miss Gold Lamé, "Your Margherita pizza, Lieutenant, enjoy. You Navy man? Officer?"

"Yes."

"I know Navy man … long time go back States, leave babysan, me. You work Saigon?"

"Yes."

"Where you work Saigon?"

"Shipyard."

"Enjoy pizza, Lieutenant, and you girlfriend."

"Thanks," he said, and she was gone to another table.

Margot said, "Now that's just sad. GI leaving that girl to fend for herself with a little baby in this mess."

"Afraid there's a lot of that going around over here. Lots of opportunity for bad behavior."

"Especially a girl like that, no doubt from a small village forced into Saigon due to the war." Margot paused to take a slice of pizza and a big bite. "Hey, this isn't bad pizza." More pauses to eat and take a swig of beer. "Charlie, do you know there are at least two types of bargirls that work these places?"

"And how do you know all this stuff?"

"Well, when I came over here last year to work for Uncle Sam, they sent us to some training sessions over by the USAID building. One was about the local society, super interesting. We spent one whole morning on bars, prostitution, drugs, and so on. Yeah, two types of bargirls. The one we just had: poor kid hustling drinks and female companionship for tips, and selling herself if she gets a buyer. If she's pretty, she makes good money … for a while."

"And the other type?"

Margot finished another piece of pizza and took another swig of 33 Export which finished her twelve-ounce bottle.

"Another beer?" Charlie asked.

Chapter Nineteen

"No frigging way … I will never go back to that restroom, ever. Okay, the other type. This type is more complex. Basically, these girls are looking for bigger prizes. Usually prettier, speak very good English, sometimes with hardly any accent unless she needs to. In general, they are more sophisticated. In fact, there is one in this bar as we speak. And she has been watching you since we sat down. This type usually goes for military officers, the higher the rank, the better. They're looking for information, secrets … treasure."

"Okay, I give up. Which girl is it?"

"All right, don't look now, but when not so obvious, you'll see a girl with big dark and dusky eyes in a sequined miniskirt and a black kind of frilly top hanging on the lieutenant colonel in the corner. Laughing with him, and rubbing against him. He is full of bourbon whisky, and his head must be spinning. She'll either walk out with him, hand-in-arm, to a private place real close by and then really try to charm him for anything important he knows, or else she'll drop him and move to the next guy. Someone like you."

"Just give me a hint of what *someone like you* means."

"Okay, she speaks very good English, no pidgin like our bargirl. I heard her speaking to the colonel in very good English when I returned from the restroom. By the way, I heard him talking about using US airpower. She is thinking you may be interesting, you look smart, you could be full of secrets, she knows you are a Navy officer, and you work at the shipyard here in Saigon."

"Whoa! How does she know that?"

"I just watched our bargirl, Miss Gold Lamé, tell Miss Dark and Dusky all about you when she left our table."

"You see a lot more than I do."

Margot said somewhat seriously, "Could it be that someone knows that you, Charlie, are supposed to keep your eyes open for suspicious activity? That would be a long shot." That made Charlie think about the comment Mr. Mi made about knowing that Commander Hargrove asked him to keep watch on Bao. He did not share that thought with Margot.

Charlie couldn't stand it any longer and gave a quick glance to that side of the bar and *boom!* There she was, gazing at him. They locked eyes for a nanosecond. She smiled and Charlie gave her a small smile in return.

"Margot, you are very good. Okay, what's the story on this girl?"

"She is either a very expensive prostitute or an agent."

"An agent?"

"An agent with a handler, probably looking for military or political secrets. She gives the handler information she's learned. He pays her a little or a lot depending on her harvest that night. He may put it with other information he gets and try to decipher it himself or send it raw to his intelligence unit."

"Margot, you just made me a little more vigilant in my actions and speech. And all it cost me was two beers and a pizza."

"I'm ready to move on, Charlie. See if you can get a good look at her on the way out, I have a bad feeling about her."

Charlie left two hundred piasters on the table as they walked out.

Chapter Twenty

The Good, the Bad and the Confused

Two more weeks went by and Charlie and Dao were buried in work that seemed to increase at an ever faster rate to meet the challenge of the Eastertide Offensive. A break came the following weekend when Charlie and Dao both got a day off.

On Saturday morning, Charlie pulled the Navy jeep into the racetrack. It was his second stop of the day. The first had been to pick up Dao and his kids and drop them at the zoo. There were no races on that Saturday, so access to the grounds was easy. He went to the infield gate and crossed the track quickly, then drove to where Binh kept their horses stabled for the day. Binh and Kim had arrived early that morning and had brought two horses they planned to race on Sunday. Bao was to join them later with a friend. "Good morning, Lieutenant," Binh greeted Charlie. "Kim is warming up Black Martin." (He pronounced the name like the French do: *Marc-Tan*, with the accent on *Tan*.)

"Good morning to you, sir! Beautiful morning."

"Ah, yes, beautiful. Every day is a gift, Lieutenant."

"You know, Binh, you certainly have gotten the use out of those combat boots. Don't think I've ever seen you without them!"

"Yes, they've served me well. I feel the closeness of my old French war friend each time I lace them up."

Charlie was surprised and delighted that Kim had named the black horse Black Martin. He went over to the track and stood by the rail as she went flying by.

Wow! Charlie thought again: *born to be on a fast moving horse!*

She was really moving out, and she didn't risk her firm hold on the reins but managed a smile and nod. One more time around and she cooled him to a trot and brought him into the family's stabling area.

"Hey, Navy boy!" she said, giving Charlie a wave and, when closer, a kiss on the cheek. "That will do till I get you alone, haha."

"When are you moving to Saigon so I can see you more often," Charlie asked, "I had to steal a jeep just to see you." Mutual laughter. "Hey, I like the name of your horse!"

"Yeah, I thought it was a good fit."

"A great fit for this big boy. Saved my life he did, you rascal," he said as he grabbed the headstall and stroked his muzzle. "I'll never be able to leave Vietnam without him. Ha!"

"What are you up to this morning?"

"Just hanging around at your service, ma'am; free till 1 p.m. when I have to pick up Dao and his kids."

"Good, I've been working this guy for forty-five minutes. He needs his breakfast. You can take him to our paddock and remove his tack, throw in some hay and grain. His water bucket should be good. Meanwhile I'll get us some coffee. I know you like your espresso!"

Chapter Twenty

Charlie did as told which kept him busy for the next fifteen minutes. Kim walked beyond the viewing stands to a coffee shop called Ca-Phe Dep (*beautiful coffee*) within a group of tiny businesses along Plantation Road. She bought two coffees and was returning when she encountered Bao and his friend.

"Oh, hi. You must be the friend that Bao is bringing over to see the horses."

Bao said, "Yes, this is Tam from our university group and her two little siblings. They wanted to see the horses. Tam, meet my sister, Kim."

"Great to meet you, Tam, and yes, we can arrange that for the kids! Charlie is in the paddock feeding the horses. I'm going there now with this coffee!" Addressing the little ones, she asked, "And what are your names?" The little ones smiled and answered, Trung and Mai; a boy and girl, respectively.

"Just follow me and I'll show you some beautiful horses." The group was all smiles as they headed to the Binh paddock.

Now this is where things got tricky. Charlie had just about finished with the horses and was looking forward to a good dark espresso. He turned and saw Kim coming with a group of people. He recognized Bao but none of the others. He smiled and waved at Kim walking with two cups of espresso, still at a distance. Then saw the girl walking with Bao. So familiar. Who the hell is she? They were almost upon him and it clicked: those big dark eyes gave her away. Margot had dissected her at the Palace. *No way out*, he thought. *I'll play it stupid for all it's worth.*

Charlie put a smile on his face and said, "You brought coffee and a crowd! Morning, Bao." Bao nodded. Charlie watched the girl closely to decipher the instant that she recognized him. He was watching the eyes … very suddenly and very slightly her eyes expanded then back to normal, all within the measure of a fraction of a second, followed by a trace of a smile. Then it was her turn to watch him closely as Kim said while handing him his coffee, "This is Bao's friend, Tam, from the University and her little brother and sister. I met them coming in by the coffee shop. The kids came to see the horses." Then, "Tam, this is my friend Charlie from the Navy shipyard."

"Nice to meet you, Tam," he said looking directly at her. "Kim's father told me Bao may have a friend coming today."

"You're American, you look familiar, have we met?" Charlie thought: *Oh she is sly and aggressive. She knows damn well where she saw me. Nothing to do but play along now. Yes, Margot, she does speak good English.*

"No, I don't think so, but I'm delighted to meet you. You speak English very well." Charlie was hoping Bao would insert himself here somewhere and lose this focus he was under.

"Aren't you the American who rode with Bao's sister on horses to escape from the NVA at An Loc?"

"Oh, that, yes, I am. Surprised you even heard about that."

"Bao mentioned it."

Kim broke in and said, "Okay, who's ready for a horse ride?" Both kids were excited and were more than ready. Binh came up to help and entertain the kids. He lifted the oldest onto the very gentle chestnut filly. Bao enjoyed leading the horse around the infield, proud of being part of this family in front of Tam. Tam and the remaining little one walked along and offered encouragement. Definitely a happy scene in this war, though less than twenty miles from here, just that morning, ARVN soldiers were dying trying to break the siege of the city of An Loc by the NVA.

It was a chance for Charlie and Kim to have some time to themselves. They sat on the covered bench by the paddock and finished their espressos. She climbed onto his lap and planted a long kiss on his mouth.

"I need to see you more often."

"What would your mother say about all this public display of affection?" Chuckles.

"She's not here and Father is way down there leading a kid around on a horse with Bao and his girlfriend."

"Girlfriend?"

"Who knows, maybe; I think he was looking at her like a girlfriend."

"Well, guess what, I'm coming to the track tomorrow to watch you ride. And we can do something then. We can take a taxi somewhere in town, if you like."

"That's more like it!"

"Yes, I need to see you more often, too." Then he told Kim he would be going on R&R in a week to visit his sister, Brigitte, in Hawaii.

Kim said, "Lucky her. Lucky you."

"Yeah, I know, but I need to see how she's doing and have a good talk with her. I'll be back in two weeks. But you know there is more and more pressure for the US to withdraw all servicemen from Vietnam. My normal rotation date should be the end of the year, but I'm starting to hear rumors of the US Command moving rotation dates up. Some guys I know have started receiving orders to return to the States as much as three months early. If that happens to me, it would put my rotation date sometime in October.

"Kim, we need to talk about stuff. Like the war, and contingencies and does your family have plans if things go haywire."

"Haywire?"

"Just a farm expression, means all messed up. What are your plans the rest of the day today?"

"Today I've got to finish preparing these horses for tomorrow, which means track time at least twice on the chestnut. She's not that good out of the gate. Father will have Bao and me on horses for practice at the gate together. We will take them both back to the farm this afternoon so they'll relax until mid-morning tomorrow. That's when we'll return to prepare for the first race at 1 p.m."

"Full day for you."

"Yeah, it's okay. I like working with both horses. They're fast learners."

"I agree with that. I experienced that a few weeks ago on our An Loc adventure!"

With that, Charlie had to leave to retrieve Dao and his gang, so he said his goodbyes and promised to be at the track before Kim raced the next day.

Meanwhile, as Kim returned to the paddock to rub down the chestnut, she noticed her father leading the two kids together on Black Martin. Bao and Tam appeared to be talking very seriously at a distance from the others. Tam and the kids had been at the track for nearly an hour, and a few minutes later Tam retrieved the kids and prepared to leave the racetrack grounds.

"I'm sorry Bao, but I need to meet my aunt at the taxi stand and return to her house in Cholon. The time is late, we must go quickly." She stopped and put her hand on his arm, offered a little private smile, and purred, "Bao, the kids had a wonderful time, thank you so much." Then hurried off.

Bao slowly approached Kim who was working on the chestnut. He was deep in thought, staring at the ground all the while, and said, "Do you think Charlie knows Tam somehow?"

"No, why would you say that?"

Chapter Twenty

"Because she said to me, 'Your sister should know something I've heard about her boyfriend, Charlie.'"

"Something she's heard about Charlie? What's that mean?"

"It's not good."

"Tell me."

"She said Charlie's a spy working with US Navy intelligence."

"What? What are you talking about?"

"That's what she said. His job is to be friendly with the local people like us to get information. Things like learning who is sympathetic to the Viet Minh. Things like that."

"I can't believe that! That just doesn't sound right." She mulled it over and said to Bao, "What do you think? Have you ever noticed anything that would even come close to that?"

"No, never noticed anything. But she was sure of it."

"How would she know this, even if it were true," she asked Bao. "She told you she was a college girl from Mi Tho, right?"

"Yes."

"That's a big accusation, Bao. How could we not know this after all the times he's been with us … with me? I'm going to see Charlie tomorrow, and I'll ask him pointblank. She added, "You know, Bao, if you don't mind my saying, there's something about that girl that seems fishy to me."

Early Sunday morning Charlie arose, dressed, and took off walking for downtown. He was heading to the USO on Nguyen Hue Street to call his sister, Brigitte. He always preferred walking to driving in the city. The streets were nearly vacant at 6 a.m. and the early morning walk was invigorating. The temperature was comfortable at that hour but expected to rise by noon, bringing a day so hot that waves of heat would be visible rising from the pavement. Charlie wondered how the horses would fare in the heat of the day's races.

He walked in the front door of the USO. It was always tricky walking in the entrance due to black market goods being offered by unsavory looking individuals pestering GIs as they entered. They were hocking tables full of things like razor blades, shaving cream, cheap cameras, cigarettes, lighters, even canned food. It was always comical to see a carton of food stamped: *A GIFT FROM THE PEOPLE OF THE UNITED STATES—NOT TO BE SOLD.* The trick was to walk fast and act like you're going past the USO, then duck in at the last moment. Same way going out. Move fast.

Charlie had planned the time of the call in a letter to Brigitte two weeks ago, and got a confirmation letter back early this week. Getting the timing right was always in question due to the limited number of open lines to the States. It could take up to an hour to connect to your party. Charlie calculated if he got the call through at 8 a.m. it would be 7 p.m. in Columbus, Ohio.

He signed in at the reception for the overseas call, then grabbed a donut and coffee at the small café run by the volunteers. He went to the lounge area to eat breakfast and watch reruns of *Bonanza* until the operator paged him. This morning he was lucky, and after thirty minutes his call went through.

In the call, Charlie disclosed to Brigitte that he was serious about Kim and was considering asking her to come back to the States with him. She was upbeat and said it didn't surprise her. She could see from his letters he was serious. She updated him on Aunt Sofia, and also she'd had good news on new leg braces that made a big improvement in her ability to walk unassisted. Charlie congratulated her and then said he'd confirmed the trip to Hawaii they had talked about.

"It will be our own private holiday for nearly two weeks, compliments of the Navy!" he said. He had made all the arrangements and

Chapter Twenty

would send her the details. "I'll meet you at Fort DeRussy in Honolulu." She was ecstatic.

The whole call lasted only twenty-one minutes. Charlie felt good about the call and it was not yet 7:30 a.m. He decided to walk up the street and attend Mass at the basilica.

The lepers hovered and prostrated themselves in his path as he stepped quickly into the vestibule while dropping coins into their reaching hands and hats. He walked to the right aisle and into a pew near his old friend Saint Michael the Archangel. Charlie's spirits were high. He knelt and asked and listened for a voice to guide him in a moment of decision over Kim. He closed his eyes for ten minutes until the music started for the 8 a.m. Mass. When he opened his eyes the church was half filled, and across the basilica near the front sat a veiled Kim and her mother.

Charlie didn't know if they had seen him, but he suspected they may have since this happened before. After Mass, Charlie went to the back of church to meet them, but Kim and Therese had evidently slipped out the side door and were nowhere to be seen.

It was only 9 a.m. when Charlie came out of the basilica, a little puzzled about where Kim and her mother had gone, but he assumed they had plans and wanted time together. He decided to grab an espresso and a Sunday paper and walk back to the shipyard. When he walked into the office he was surprised to find Margot busy typing some briefing papers.

"What the devil are you doing in here on such a fine day off, Margot?"

"Just some extra work the captain wanted."

"He's here today?"

"Oh, no, no, he doesn't do Sundays. So what about you, Charlie, how's your weekend off going?"

"Good so far. Called my sis this morning, she's fine. Took in 8 a.m. Mass at the basilica. Hey, here's something you may be interested in. I was helping Kim at the racetrack yesterday morning and guess who I saw?"

"Willie Shoemaker?"

"Ha! Good one! No, I saw our friend from the pizza place the other night."

"What friend? Who?"

"You know, that girl with the dark eyes working the colonel."

"You mean Suzie? The one I said who was looking you over?"

"One and the same. She came with two little siblings, so she said, to see and ride the horses. I was introduced to her, different name but same girl. Introduced as 'Tam.'"

"Did she recognize you?"

"Of course, but she didn't let on that she remembered me from the Palace. Nor did I. But she wasn't shy about saying I looked familiar."

"Hang on Charlie, I need to make a call." Margot went into Captain Eagleton's office and shut the door. She came out five minutes later and said, "Okay, don't get mad at me, Strickland, but I've got some collateral duties around here that you don't know about. But I'm going to explain to you right now."

"I just talked to your friend Commander Hargrove. He said we need to bring you up to speed."

"We?"

"Yeah, like I said I'm going to explain." She took a breath. "Remember all this is SECRET. I've actually been working with Hargrove for the last six months. I really am an administrative assistant to the captain, but kind of like your situation, I was recruited by Hargrove to help out in NIS. In fact, that's what I'm doing here today. So, yes, I'm

Chapter Twenty

working for the Naval Intelligence Service. Much more involved than you are, I might add."

"Well, you sure make a good sleuth," Charlie said in a friendly manner. "I didn't suspect a thing at the pizza place the other night. Even your story about all your training over by the USAID building!"

"Oh, yeah. Sorry 'bout that. Actually I did do some training over there so it wasn't a complete lie. Thanks for not crucifying me. Okay, here's what I know about Miss Suzie. She's someone we've been watching. Actually we're pretty sure she's a Viet Minh agent and has a handler. She's been seen getting into a white Mazda. We know she's definitely been meeting with the Viet Minh. How did she get involved with the racetrack?"

Charlie explained what he knew. "I was told she met Bao at the University and found out his family was involved with racing. May have invited herself, for all I know. Maybe it was innocent. She just wanted the kids to see the horses. That was about it. I left before she and the kids left."

Charlie had some other thoughts on Tam's visit to the track but didn't want Binh's family to become involved on just his own suspicions, so he kept them to himself. He thanked Margot for letting him know she was with Hargrove, and went to his billet. There he did some personal correspondence and after a bite for lunch, left for the track.

Chapter Twenty-one

Heartache

The weather forecast was turning out to be correct. The air was still and blazingly hot, and it was only midday. Charlie thought of the horses running in the heat of the afternoon. This morning's *Saigon Post* carried a small story of a kind of special "French Day" today at the racetrack. A special purse would be offered sponsored by The French-Vietnam Association and a sports club in Saigon.

His taxi dropped Charlie at the front of the track grounds. He showed his ticket, walked in, and noticed many of the old French population in the stands and milling around the area. He walked away from the crowd to the chain-link fence surrounding the track to view the activity. Some horses were out there warming.

He immediately recognized Kim in her white and jade silks posting on the big black horse at a fast trot on the outside of the track. He watched as she rounded into the stretch. He could see little puffs of

Chapter Twenty-one

dust with each hoofbeat, nostrils flaring on Black Martin with each breath as the animal approached him, head held high and ears pricked forward. The horse was lathered already, forty minutes before race time. Charlie appreciated once again the huge energy contained in the powerful animal and the skill and strength required to control him to a winning performance in a professional horse race.

He gave a wave and a smile, but the rider kept a strict countenance and forward concentration as they passed by. For just an instant, they were so close he could see details of the heel of her black riding boot from which he had carved mud only weeks before. Horse and rider swooshed by, no more than three feet from his person, and were gone. For the second time today, Charlie was disappointed there was no communication from Kim. There was more than thirty minutes before race time, so he crossed the track quickly to wish Kim good luck.

Kim brought the animal in a few minutes later to cool him and let him have a limited drink of water. Charlie was waiting for her, walked to her, and said, "Good morning, Kim, I saw you in church this morning. I went out the front and waited but you must have gone another way. I didn't see you afterwards."

"Yes, I was there with my mother."

When he saw her face, that she did not look at him, and heard her tone, Charlie sensed immediately something was wrong.

"Hey ... Kim, what's wrong?"

Kim answered slowly and rather defiantly. "What's wrong? Well ... there's a line that I'm having a hard time crossing for you, and I don't want to discuss it right now. I have a large purse race I'm getting ready to ride. I have a life of my own, apart from you, in case you haven't noticed. We need to talk when I'm finished with this race. Privately. Let's meet at my friend Camille's place later at 3 p.m. It's private, remember the place?"

"Sure, of course. I'll be there, do you need a ride?"

"No."

"But I don't understand ... "

She interrupted him. "We'll talk later." With that, she turned the horse over to a handler, turned on her heel, and went to relax before the race.

Charlie was stunned. He was left with a big question mark in his mind. He thought: *She is really ticked. I must have screwed up in a horrible way. I've known her nearly six months, I've never seen this side of her. What the hell did I do?*

Charlie decided to go to the stands and watch the race from his ticketed seat, which was a good one. He hurried across the track and up into the stands. He tried to understand what Kim was so upset about. One thing was sure: it was something to do with him. He tried to think what happened since last he saw her the day before. He remembered that Kim was looking forward to spending time with him after she raced today. He recalled that the girl introduced to him as Tam was still at the track when he left yesterday. What changed? Was Tam involved?

Charlie turned his attention to the race. The horses were coming out onto the track and parading past the stands for the betting crowd to take a final look. Last call for placing bets was announced. Charlie looked at the field of six horses. There were two big horses: Black Martin and a big four-year-old sorrel filly. Full of energy, the sorrel pranced across the front of the stands and caused a commotion among the French crowd.

The jockey wore the tri-color silks and waved uncharacteristically to the crowd. The four remaining horses were unknowns; their records were skimpy. Two of them had a couple of wins, but mostly were wild cards.

Chapter Twenty-one

All horses loaded uneventfully into the starting gate. The bell rang out and they were off. One of the unknown four shot out to the rail and in a burst of speed took the lead, cutting off Black Martin in the process. Kim pulled him up to avoid a collision, then a second horse did the same.

The big black horse took it all in stride, content to stay in the rear by the rail where Kim had a good view and could judge the performance of the field. She was confident her horse had a wealth of energy and power in reserve. The sorrel was hugging the rail in front of Kim. Going into the clubhouse turn, Kim realized the pace was too fast for this hot day, and unless those four were super animals they would melt away quickly and her only rival would be the young sorrel filly.

At the beginning of the backstretch, the sorrel made her move and in a flashy show of speed moved to the outside, taking the lead on the rail as the four started to fade. Kim thought: *That jock will pay for that silly waste of energy.* Kim, knowing she had a lot of horse under her, gave him rein, passed the four quickly on the outside, then pulled up to settle in on the right hindquarter of the sorrel just off the rail on the backstretch. From then it was a two-horse race.

Kim began a controlled increase of Black Martin's speed, which forced the tiring filly to run faster and faster. The filly began to labor and, feeling her horse wanting to run, Kim let Black Martin continue to push the sorrel through the far turn. Down the stretch she gave him his head and he easily passed the filly, and was soon leading by five lengths.

She crouched low and spoke to her horse in a gentle voice. "Di don gio, nguoi dep cua toi" (*Go catch the wind, my beauty*), and he responded with blazing speed. The sorrel's jockey angrily whipped his horse hard on her flanks, first one side, then the other, though the animal was exhausted and falling far behind. To the delight of the crowd, the big black horse won by nine lengths. Even the French were amazed at the show for their special holiday.

Patrons applauded in a standing ovation as Kim cooled down her horse in a trot around the track. In the winner's circle, the Memorial Award was presented to Sunstone Farm owner and trainer Nguyen Binh Li, jockey Nguyen Kim Li, and Black Martin (printed on the French-Viet race card as "Mar-tin Noir").

In the stands, Charlie was proud and impressed with Kim and wished he had someone to tell, "That's my girlfriend on the winning horse!" He folded the race card and slipped it into his chest pocket as a souvenir. He wondered, *I think she's still my girlfriend.*

Kim jumped off the horse and gave him to the handlers. She went to her father and kissed him. "Thanks, Father, we did it! He was a good buy, wasn't he?"

"Yes, he is a very good horse. After all he was one of two who brought you and the Lieutenant home safely to us. We have a lot to thank him for. He hugged her and said, "You did a fine job of reading the field and maneuvering him to victory, Kim. You deserve half of the winnings. We'll put it away for your university funds."

"Thanks, Father."

Kim was sitting in the back of the small closed-in patio of Camille's apartment staring into space when Charlie came in. She was calm but seemed weary, "Sit down, Charlie, Camille won't be back until late tonight. There's a glass of tea if you wish."

"Thanks. And congratulations on your win." Charlie sat down and picked up the glass of tea.

Chapter Twenty-one

"Thank you." Kim looked directly at Charlie and took a deep breath, "Charlie, have you been spying on me and my family, and then reporting to some commander? I don't remember his name."

Charlie was shocked by the direct accusation. He felt like he'd been hit in the face with a two-by-four. Still, he resolved to think before he spoke, and wanted to remain calm. He knew of course what she was referring to. And he knew the commander was obviously Hargrove. He had accused Hargrove of asking him to do exactly what Kim was now expressing. Nevertheless, he didn't think it was right or even accurate to acknowledge what she was referring to. For one thing, the conversation he'd had with Hargrove was SECRET. And for another, he had never actually spied on her or anyone in her family. He was not going to look for trouble, and only if he observed something that intentionally crossed the line of causing injury to the US or its allies would he report it. He felt that complied with the spirit of Hargrove's request.

"What?" he said. "What are you talking about? Why would you say that?"

"Never mind where that comes from right now, it's a simple question: Yes or no?"

"The answer is no. I have not spied on you or your family. But I'm interested in why you asked that. Something has obviously disturbed you. Did someone say that or insinuate that?"

Kim ignored the question. "Did you know the girl that came to the track with Bao yesterday? I heard her say you looked familiar to her."

"I didn't know her or was ever introduced to her before yesterday. But I did see her before, just once. She was working as a bargirl on Tu Do Street when I saw her last Friday."

"On Tu Do Street?"

"That's right. Friday afternoon, I went to the Emperor's Palace for pizza with Margot, you know, our secretary. I saw her there, Tam, if that is her name. She was a bargirl there. I didn't talk to her, but I'm sure it was her. I'm sure she recognized me, too. I remember because she was with an American colonel at a table facing ours, and she kept looking at Margot and me. Yesterday, I thought it was inappropriate of her to start a conversation with me that could have led to embarrassment for others. Others such as Bao or your father, so I didn't acknowledge her."

"What do you mean, 'If Tam was her name?'"

"She was referring to herself as 'Suzie' at the bar."

"Okay, yes, I am disturbed. Tam or … 'Suzie' told my brother, Bao, that you are spying on our family. Why would she do that?"

Charlie said, "I can't answer that, but I'm sure you understand that I'm an officer in the United States Navy, and officially an advisor to the Republic of Vietnam, and I'm obliged to stand alongside South Vietnam against our common enemy, North Vietnam. That means if I come across enemy military information that could hurt South Vietnam, I have no choice but to report it to some higher authority. I mean, that's what everyone in the US military service must do. I don't think that's a revelation to you. I don't have any idea what Tam's motives are. I can only say that I have never spied or reported anything on you or your family."

Neither said anything for a while, but Charlie could see Kim was trying to draw conclusions from all that she now knew. Charlie said, "What do *you* think about her and what she told Bao?"

"I don't know how I feel. I thought about it all night. I couldn't sleep. I was trying to think in my mind how I felt about you before she said all this. You and I have been through so much together. I meant

Chapter Twenty-one

it when I said I loved you. I trusted you deeply. I don't know anything about her, except what Bao told me. But she told Bao she was so sure she was right. It bothered me."

Kim took a deep breath and continued. "It bothered me because a little bit of me was scared that what happened to my friend Camille would happen to me."

"What do you mean?"

"Camille dated an American army officer for nearly a year, with plans to marry. One day he abruptly went home, no explanation. He left and she stayed. That was a year ago, and she still has not recovered."

"I feel bad for her," Charlie said. "That's not right. But that's not me; I don't work that way. I hope you know that."

"I do know that, but we all have secrets. Secrets that we hold close. I have secrets, too, that you don't know about and perhaps never will. All I'm saying is the things Tam said came out of the blue with no explanation, and it's bothered me. How would she even know anything about you?"

"I have no idea *how* she would know or even *if* she knows anything about me. But, I know how I feel about you: I love you and I trust you. I was thinking we could have a future … I still do." He could feel himself getting hot. "And I definitely know how I feel about Tam, or whatever her name is: I wouldn't trust her as far as I could throw her. My belief is that anyone laughing while pouring whisky into a senior army officer so drunk he can't stand and talking in mock pidgin English to sound cute has dubious intentions. And I don't condone the army officer, either." Charlie thought, *Dammit, I'm getting all riled up. Cool down, Strickland, you're not talking to Eagleton.* He said, "I'm sorry, Kim, I didn't mean to raise my voice." He drank a sip of tea and took a deep breath.

They sat quietly for a while and finally Kim said, "You're still going on R&R in about a week, right? Did you decide to see your sister?"

"Yes, I'll be gone for about two weeks. I need to spend time with Brigitte. As siblings, we've always been close."

Kim said, "Maybe it would be good to be apart for a while, even if you weren't going on R&R. I need time to think about my life and how I really feel about everything that's happened to me in the last six months. If we have a future, the next six months would require large changes and sacrifices for both of us."

Her words startled Charlie. It made him feel this could be the end of something he held so dearly. Nevertheless he agreed with Kim and said. "Perhaps we should, especially if you feel that something doesn't fit quite right. I can understand that. If we do have a future together, yes, it would require sacrifice on both our parts. You would likely bear the largest burden of changes. And much depends on this crazy war.

"But I'm going to stay optimistic. We can take some time off, but I like us as a couple, and I'm one who believes if there's a will, things will work out. The issue of trust is so important. It's kind of like your faith, you either trust someone or you don't. It can't be halfway. You have to feel completely comfortable. We come from such different worlds, and yet I believe we have so much in common."

Then he stood and said, "Well, I must go. I'll be busy tomorrow and the rest of the coming week in boat testing. So I guess this is goodbye for now. Should I call you when I return?"

"Of course you should. Be safe until then, Charlie. Oh wait! Here is a small gift for Brigitte; just something I did with a needle and some thread. It's traditional Vietnamese. Be sure to tell her I said hello."

"I will. Goodbye, Kim."

Chapter Twenty-two

R&R in Hawaii

A week later, Charlie took a taxi to Camp Alpha to out-process for his Hawaii flight. At 9 a.m., he walked up the rollaway stairs to the PANAM 747-100 at Tan Son Nhut Airbase. From the platform at the top of the stairs he looked around the base and saw the sky darkening in the west. It added to the gloom he felt as he entered the aircraft and found his seat. The situation in Vietnam was so fluid by July, 1972, that one didn't know for sure if he would be coming back. He left Vietnam that morning with a heavy heart, knowing it could be the last he would be with Kim. Was he being realistic about bringing her to America and expecting her to leave all that she knew and all that she had known in her life? Her close-knit family and all her friends, her dream of higher education in a professional school of art, her respected position in professional horse racing and the country that she loved. And the very real possibility that she may never be reunited with any of that again.

He concluded she certainly was entitled to think long and hard about that decision. The life event on which she had sought her mother's opinion had happened: she had fallen in love with an American serviceman and he with her. She had to decide, if Charlie asked, would she go or would she stay.

She knew deep down Charlie was not the American her friend Camille had dealt with. Charlie was basically an honorable person. Even her father said as much. They would talk it out in detail, and all of the changes that were continuing to evolve in Vietnam would be considered by both of them. She knew Charlie would talk with her parents about all of it. That was one of the things she liked about him: they talked things over and trusted each other's opinion. Kim knew one thing more. Charlie would come back with his mind made up. She needed to have her decision ready.

The more Charlie thought about it, the more he began to realize that the disruption that Tam had caused with her few words to Bao would have little to no effect on their relationship or decisions in life. Their decisions would be based on solid values and trust.

His aircraft landed in Honolulu International Airport at 10:35 a.m. He flew all day and landed an hour later! How does that work? Time zones, jet stream, speed of the aircraft, and so forth and so on. He took a Navy bus to Fort DeRussy where the servicemen met their loved ones. Brigitte was there in a wheelchair. She pulled herself up and they held each other tightly.

"Hey, sis!"

"Hey, Brother Strickland! How was the flight?"

"No idea, been sleeping sixteen hours! How 'bout you?"

"Great flight, two segments: Columbus to Chicago, Chi-town to Honolulu, both good."

Chapter Twenty-two

Brigitte had come the day before and got the room. They verified her return United flight before they left the airport. They went to the hotel, dumped their stuff, then left and were on the go for three days until they wore down and started to do what they came for: relax on the beach. That's when all the personal stuff came out for both of them.

Brigitte had all good news: Aunt Sofia was surviving, actually thriving with a college kid living with her. Brigitte's legs were improving. She had set a goal to be completely independent. Her doctor was a very positive one and had her working hard. Studies were good. Two more years of college and she'd have her degree in microbiology. Things were going good and getting better in Columbus Town.

Charlie had written to Brigitte so often that much of this trip was just about spending time together—and understanding the unspoken communications that passed between the two of them. Most of his news was already known, or she'd gotten the gist of it over the months. These were topics like the racetrack, or the successes of his projects with Dao, and his descriptions of the country and its people. She knew the big topic he wanted to discuss was Kim. There was no one in Vietnam he could trust like Brigitte to expose his deepest feelings about Kim. Brigitte would not judge nor would she preach.

And expose them he did. From the first meeting at the track accident to the escape from An Loc, to the ache in his heart he felt when he was not with her, to the stunning and heartbreaking conversation they had before he left. He was worn out just going through it all but was relieved that he did. He finished by saying, "I've labored with this situation and now I need to make a decision before my return to Vietnam next week."

Brigitte was a good listener, and she listened to what the words said and what the eyes and face said as he talked of Kim. She said, "You are a good man, Charlie. An honorable man. You have your values intact. And from all you've told me of Kim, you've described a person with her values intact as well. You and me and Kim, we are all young. And this is one of those big moments in young lives that set a direction for the rest of our lives. It's one of the few that we have control over. You've spoken of Kim in such heartfelt terms, Charlie. If you could only hear yourself. I think you've already made your decision. You've listened to your heart."

Chapter Twenty-three

Back to Vietnam

Brigitte left Hawaii on an evening flight from Honolulu bound for Columbus, Ohio, via Chicago after a wonderful two-week vacation with Charlie. Charlie left to return to Vietnam the following day. It was dusk when he left and he flew all night. The aircraft made a quick stop to refuel at Guam Island, then continued on. The sun was beginning to peek up above the eastern horizon as the Boeing 747 lined up for final approach to Tan Son Nhut Airbase when the pilot announced the airbase was under a mortar attack. Charlie cringed. That just added multiple issues to his life.

The pilot swung the big plane northward and twenty minutes later it was banking to line up to the 10,000-foot runway at Cam Ranh Bay. The landing was uneventful except for a long, long taxi of forty-five minutes on the sprawling flat coastal base. He was back on Vietnam soil.

The three hundred-plus cranky passengers exited the plane and made their way into and around the small facility, searching for restrooms and coffee. This was a commercial flight, a mixture of military and civilians. Charlie knew it would be hours before new plans would be made and executed to get all these people back to Saigon. In the meantime he found a small office for NAVFAC, a Navy facility, and they helped him get through by phone to the Navy Construction Bureau at the Saigon shipyard. Thirty minutes later Margot was on the line.

"Hey, Margot!"

"Welcome back, Charlie!"

"Thanks, it's great to be back."

"Liar, ha-ha! Hey, we had a little bit of excitement around here this morning. VC messed up the long runway pretty badly early this morning. They still haven't called 'All Clear' yet for people at the base. It's going to be a while before the runway is fixed, several big craters, pretty accurate this time."

"Anything else hit besides the base?"

"Yeah, actually several mortars fell on Plantation Road; it's blocked. VC just overshot the base evidently. Actually, it's near the racetrack. That hasn't happened for a while."

Charlie frowned.

"Anyone hurt?"

"Yes, I'm sorry to say, the word is that two boys leading horses down Plantation Road were hit. One was killed along with the horse. The other is critical, in the hospital."

"Have you heard from anyone from Binh's family? Do you know if they were at the track?"

Margot replied, "Haven't heard. Was going to ask Dao to see if he could contact someone. His wife communicates with Kim sometimes."

Chapter Twenty-three

"Thanks, Margot. My guess is earliest I'll be back is tomorrow. If you could pass that on to the captain, I would appreciate it. They want their phone back, gotta go, and take care."

While Charlie was landing in Cam Ranh Bay, a white Mazda four-door pulled up in front of Tam's mother's house. A Vietnamese gentleman in his forties wearing leisure attire rapped on the fragile door. Tam answered immediately.

"Tam, gather your things, and your mother and the two children. You must go underground for a while. I'll be back in an hour to retrieve all of you and only the belongings we can fit in the boot of this car."

"Why? What's going on?"

"You've been blown. They know about you; it's just a matter of time before they find you here. Plantation Road is blocked. That may delay them a bit."

"How was I blown?"

"You talked too much. You said something to the people at the racetrack that made them suspicious. Now the government police and the Americans are after you. You're lucky we have a safe house for you. Tell your mother she's going to an apartment with running water. That will make it easier; she will be pleased."

"I need more time to get my mother ready."

"One hour. If you're not ready in one hour, I'll drive away. It's not safe here. You, or I, could end up a political prisoner in Poulo Condore."

Tam drew a quick short breath of alarm at the mention of the notorious island prison in the South China Sea off the coast of South Vietnam. The thought of Poulo Condore frightened her into action.

After the man had gone, Tam stuffed clothing into three bags: the kids' things, her mother's, and her own. She took another bag and put personal items, toiletries, and a couple of toys and books for the kids. She also packed her most valuable items which she'd been carrying for years: a statue of the Blessed Virgin received at First Holy Communion, a photo of her deceased father, some photos of each child, and her vase for joss sticks.

She moved her mother onto the homemade transporter and wheeled her to the door. The two kids waited there with juice boxes she had planned for dinner. She was ready in forty-five minutes.

Her handler showed up in one hour and helped her load all into his car and they were gone in five minutes. They drove in silence to a first-floor apartment deep into Cholon, the Chinese business district within the disordered maze of humanity in Saigon. They moved in quickly. The apartment was a palace compared to where they had been living. It consisted of a bathroom with running water, two tiny bedrooms, and a kitchen and sitting room.

Out of earshot of her mother, he spoke to her. "I would advise you to go off the grid, Tam. You should lay low for an undetermined amount of time. You need to change your appearance. I recommend you cut your hair short and maybe a different style. Minimize makeup and the like. Your days of glamour will need to be put on hold for a while."

He added, "You have been a valuable asset and provided useful information. The movement wants to keep you. There will be tasks that you can do to serve while here. I'll contact you in a couple of days."

He handed her a packet with some money and contact codes and numbers. "I need to leave lest they see my car. It's probably known to them by now. I'll have another next time I contact you."

Chapter Twenty-three

He climbed into the Mazda and was gone.

She spoke to the family, "It's our new home, it will be much better than before, and maybe I'll have more time at home with everyone. Look, we even have real furniture and beds. I got paid today, so after dark, I'll go out and get some dinner for all of us."

That night, after they had eaten and the streets were dark and all were asleep, and the back streets and alleys of Cholon echoed with only the footfalls of the Chinese mafia, she lay in bed and said a silent prayer: "Father in Heaven, please let me meet that nice boy I met at the University someday. I'll tell him I'm sorry for what I said, and perhaps he'll forgive me and if I'm lucky, someday we can have a real life."

Finally, two days after landing at Cam Ranh Bay, Charlie was able to get a seat back to Saigon. He had slept two nights in the Cam Ranh Airport, thankful he was able to get a cot from his Navy friends at their office. The same plane he came in on left at 9 a.m. bound for Saigon. Charlie was eager to get back to his quarters, get cleaned up, and put on some fresh clothes for a change.

He arrived at Tan Son Nhut at 9:30 a.m. and called Margot. I got a call from Margot a few minutes later and took the gray Navy jeep out to the airport. Charlie had a big grin on his face as he jumped into the jeep. "Never thought I'd be saying 'So good to be back in Saigon,' but here I am. Cam Ranh Bay's not much for serving 350 hungry passengers, though. I'm starving; I'll buy breakfast or brunch, whatever. Got time for Kenny's?"

"Always got time for Kenny's."

We walked in to Kenny's American, no lunch crowd yet.

Kenny called out, "Howdy, fellers, coffee?"

"Very black and lots of it," Charlie answered. "Does Josie still do those buttermilk pancake thingies with black market Bisquick?"

"Absolutely. Just got a new shipment of half a dozen boxes in yesterday. Straight from the kid alongside the flower stalls on Nguyen Hue. He's pretty reliable, don't know how he does it."

"Thank the Lord for him," Charlie said. "That's what I want, big stack."

I told Kenny I'd take a small stack, then asked Charlie about R&R.

Charlie dived into his food and drink. Between gulps he said, "I had a great R&R. I did some hard thinking and deciding on things that are important to me. I'm going to ask Kim to marry me. Don't care where or when, but I'm going to do my best to get her out of Vietnam with me. I truly believe if I don't, I'll be sorry for the rest of my life. You know it's a funny thing. I realized this morning that my mother did the same thing when she was about my age. In France, during World War II, married my real father there. I told you that he was killed over there when I was only an infant. I don't remember a thing, of course.

"By the way, Brigitte is fine; she's in total support of Kim and me. Sends her best to you."

Charlie inhaled the pancakes and went back to the shipyard. He fell asleep on the way. He slept the rest of the day and that night. The next day, he was good as new.

Chapter Twenty-four

Reunion

I met with Charlie early the next day to talk about things at the office since his absence. I mentioned I'd heard that more and more of our colleagues were getting early releases from Vietnam. After that, I headed out with Danh to a housing project at Nha Be.

Charlie looked up Margot and queried her about Kim. She knew nothing and suggested Dao. He went to the machine shop where Dao was working with a welder on motor mount brackets for a patrol boat.

"Hey, welcome back American buddy!" Dao said.

"It's great to be back and see all you characters again," Charlie said, honestly. This had become his trusted support environment.

Dao said, "Let's go into the blueprint room and talk. I take it you haven't seen Kim yet?"

"No, not yet, but you say that as if there's something wrong."

"No, not wrong, but Kim and Phuong have talked, and something is up about the girl Kim's family met named Tam. Kim wanted to tell you when you got back. I'm just the messenger. I'm supposed to pass on that Kim is staying with her friend Camille tonight, if you get back and it's convenient."

"Thanks, Dao, I'll try to get there."

Charlie got updated on the boat projects they were working on, and as he went around and discussed the projects he noticed something a little different in the shop's general demeanor. He questioned Dao about it.

"Yeah, I can feel it, too. You know, around here the guys are painfully aware of the ceasefire talks between Kissinger and North Vietnam's Le Duc Tho."

"I'm sure," Charlie agreed.

Dao continued, "It's in the headlines every day now. Most believe your President's need to finalize an agreement is driven by the timing of the American presidential election."

Charlie said, "Wouldn't you say that was a good thing in general, for both sides, anyway?"

"It's a good thing, unless Kissinger gives too much away just to have an agreement before the election. That's what our president, Nguyen Van Thieu, is fearful of. People are nervous about that. And then there's also a push on our side's part to get as much as we can completed to build defenses for the worst case agreement. They're working many hours. I'm sure you know, Charlie, we depend greatly on America. Just as the North depends on their big allies. Any agreement, we believe, will require many Americans leaving." A pause, then he said, "These things are bringing a more serious atmosphere to the work environment around here."

Chapter Twenty-four

"Yes, I understand. Has to be tough." Charlie and Dao then reviewed the status of all the projects they had in play and was updated on the reports of the boats they had operating at Wunder Beach. Afterward, Charlie went back to the office to address the pile of paperwork that accumulated while he was gone.

By noon, Danh and I returned from Nha Be. Charlie and I talked a bit about what Dao had said about the demeanor in the shop. I told Charlie that I had noticed that same seriousness in trips to the Delta while he was gone.

"The natives are getting restless."

"My issues with travel to get back here from Oahu don't seem all that important compared to what these guys are facing."

Charlie left work at 6 p.m., walked up to Hong Thap Tu, grabbed a taxi and went directly to meet Kim at Camille's apartment. He walked up the three steps to the landing and rang the bell. The door opened immediately. Kim was there with a huge welcoming smile on her face.

"Saw the taxi; hoping it was you!" She was wearing a coral Asian smock and baggy black sateen trousers. He could see her small tan bare feet on the finished bamboo floor. She had a jaunty air about her that exuded happiness and love of life. Charlie was not expecting this and thought, *Now this is the Kim I remember; she's back!* He was still standing at the door when she said almost comically, "Well, come in, Lieutenant!"

He crossed the threshold and before he could get the door closed, she jumped into his arms and pulled herself up so high that Charlie had to catch her and hold her from falling. He was amazed at how light she was. Her constant kisses muffled his words of "God, how I missed you!" as they proceeded to get reacquainted.

Sometime later, she took him by the hand to the small love seat and said, "Sit down, Charlie, I fixed some tea and snacks. Tell me all about R&R. How is Brigitte?"

"Brigitte? She's fine, and she says thanks for the kind gift."

Charlie told her everything that occurred in the two weeks.

Then she said, "Charlie I must tell you something. I was upset when you left. The issue of Tam befuddled me and I hadn't time to think it through. In the last two weeks I've looked at it from a different perspective, and I realized it couldn't have any effect on you and me. Now I feel I should have laughed it off. I couldn't understand where Tam was coming from. Bao and I talked and we were both shocked at what she had told Bao. None of it made sense. Why would she even know you? Maybe *she* was a spy.

"We talked about it, and Bao said his friend, Mi, knows more about such things. Sometimes I think my brother is so naïve, but perhaps it's best in this case. Mi checked discreetly with elements he knows. The word is she's a poor kid that got mixed up with an agency that trades sex for information on the war. Not even sure which side she works for, but probably the Viet Minh. I haven't told Bao and don't plan to."

"That's wise."

She said, "Bao still has a crush on her. They actually have many interests in common. But now there's a new twist. Bao said she's disappeared. She no longer comes to the political discussions at the University. And she's dropped out of the University. No one has seen her. It's all very mysterious."

"It could be she is just a casualty of war, part of the many who've become refugees to escape violence in her village. They are forced into a situation to survive and feed their families. She's a smart and attractive girl and valuable to unscrupulous elements for prostitution or other high risk and dangerous work. She may have been forced to take this work to survive and feed her kids. Bringing her kids to see the horses may have been her legitimate attempt at trying to bring a little normalcy to their lives."

"Her kids? Do you think those were her kids?"

"Just a guess, I don't have any idea, but it seemed she treated them as such. Their ages seemed that it's more likely they were her kids than siblings."

"Yes, maybe. But the whole matter of Tam really doesn't concern me or how I think of you, Charlie. Just wanted you to know that."

"That's wonderful, because I have something I want to give you from Hawaii." From his breast pocket, he retrieved a thin elegant black box the size of a very thin cigarette pack. He opened it to expose a beautiful pearl ring from the Island of Kauai and said, "I've discovered I love you so much that I don't want to live without you. I want to marry you, Kim. Will you have me?"

"A thousand yeses, Charlie!"

Then she threw her arms about him and proved it.

They went to a restaurant that night to celebrate their promises to each other. They chose Piccolo's on the City Wharf because of the fond memories of their first date. That night, they decided the first thing they must do is together talk with Kim's parents about their future plans.

Chapter Twenty-five

Goodbye Tam

Bao walked down tree-lined Pasteur Street on his way to meet Mi for their discussion meeting at the University. He was especially excited for the meeting because they were going to debate the issues of the Cease-fire Agreement being discussed by the government and compare that against the form of democracy Bao had proposed to the group. Pasteur Street was named after the French doctor who invented the process of pasteurization. It was one of the most beautiful streets in the city, a wide boulevard that transported one mentally to afternoon walks in Paris on the *Champs-Élysées*. In the shadows of the large old trees a small girl was coming toward him. His heart began pounding when he realized it was Tam.

He had not seen her since the racetrack with the little ones. She was alone and looking straight at him and smiling. She passed through some shadows then looked around and stopped in a dark area. She let him come to her. When in front of her, she said in a low sincere voice, "Hello, Bao, I'm so glad to see you."

Bao was as unsettled as a schoolboy, searching for words and coming up with only, "Hello, Tam. Are you coming to the meeting today?"

"No, I can't today. I have to work."

There was a pause then she smiled at him and said, "I wanted to see you, though." Another pause and she said in a contrite voice, "Bao, I'm sorry, Bao."

"Sorry? For what?"

"For saying all those things about your sister's American boyfriend. It was not right for me to do that. I hope you will forgive me someday." Her big dark eyes had gone misty.

"Actually, I won't be able to come to the meetings anymore. I have to work. I also disenrolled from the University because of my job."

This was not the Tam who appeared some six weeks ago at the political meeting so sure of herself and ready to defend her beliefs. This was a tired, mentally (and possibly physically) abused person.

"But I wanted to see you, so you would know about me. I hope we can still be friends. Maybe someday we'll meet again. I would like to get to know you better someday."

"Sure, of course. Me, too."

"Well, I must go now; it was nice to see you. I'm late for work." She laughed a little. "Goodbye, Bao." She looked around. Her constant furtive glances alarmed him. Then she quickly moved close to him, touched the side of his face, and said, "Take care, Bao."

With a confused look, Bao said, "Yeah, see you…good luck with your new job."

She looked around again and said, "Thanks!"

Then she abruptly crossed the street, walked back down the opposite side, and was gone. Bao was left standing there. He may have been naïve, but he was at the same time very intelligent. He thought to himself: *She's been forced, in some way or by someone, to the other side. What a waste. Damn this stupid war and all those who support it!*

He was beginning to believe some of the things that he and Kim had discussed late that Sunday night three weeks ago: Why does it seem in war that the worst misfortune befalls the best people?

Chapter Twenty-six

Getting Permission

Charlie rapped on Captain Eagleton's door and said, "Good morning, Captain." The Captain, of course, continued pretending he was reading something very important until the required time had passed. Then he said, "Come in, Lieutenant Strickland." He seemed in a better mood than normal. "Yes, sit down, I have here some orders for you I received late yesterday."

"Orders, sir? What type of orders?"

"Orders for your rotation date. I'm sure you will be looking forward to that. Most people are." Charlie was conditioned to take the last comment as a slight.

"But my normal rotation is January, '73. It's only August."

"By that time, you'll be out of the Navy and well into a new career, I imagine. The force levels in all the services are being reduced as we phase out of Vietnam. And the Peace Talks. Well, they're starting to move. Nixon is pushing to get an agreement before the election, so he'd like to see in-country force reductions speeded up."

Good news to many, but not necessarily to Charlie. As the captain handed the set of orders to Charlie, he summarized: "You are to report to Camp Alpha for out-processing and transportation back to the States by 1 October, 1972. And then to Yerba Buena Island, San Francisco, by 4 October, 1972, for release from active duty."

Charlie had known this could happen, but he didn't expect it so soon. That was only five weeks from now. Would there be enough time for the kind of wedding Kim wanted at the basilica? He hadn't done more than a cursory look at what was involved in getting her out of the country.

He quickly reasoned that the captain's upbeat mood might offer an opportunity to broach the subject of Charlie's intention to marry Kim and take her to the States. He knew that a recommendation from one's command officer carried a good deal of weight for a visa approval, but he was also aware of the old adage: The wants and needs of the Navy don't necessarily match the wants and needs of the individual. Nevertheless, he thought: *No time like the present to draw battle lines.* Charlie said, "Captain, perhaps this would be an appropriate time to inform you of my intention to marry a young lady I've been seeing here in Vietnam. And hopefully taking her with me when I finish my duty here. I understand that one's command approval is highly desirable before that process can begin. I was hoping to get your approval soon."

The captain sat and stared at Charlie and said nothing until it was starting to become embarrassing. Charlie stared back at him, maintaining eye contact and trying to maintain a pleasant look on his face. Finally, the captain said, "A Vietnamese girl, I take it?"

"Yes, sir."

Chapter Twenty-six

"You know my feelings on that subject. You would be making a big mistake, son, if you married one of those *Veet girls*. Can't you see she's playing you to get out of this godforsaken country and get citizenship in our great country? How stupid can one be? Why, hell, she may be a communist herself, for all you know."

"Captain, she's definitely not a communist. Her family has supported South Vietnam over many years, as I've mentioned to you before."

"I told you not to get mixed up with those people, those girls. Nothing but trouble."

"Sir, I will take full responsibility for my actions."

"Well, damn right you will, but that makes no difference to me. I won't approve of it, sooner or later or ever! I won't be a party to any of that dirty business. You're excused, Lieutenant."

Charlie could think of no one he hated more than Captain Eagleton, but he dared not to lose his temper.

Danh and I had just returned with the team from installing a water catchment system in a place called Ha Tien over in Long Xuyen province, as Charlie was coming out of the captain's office. I saw him and rather under my breath said, "Whoa, you brave soul, coming out of there! I generally avoid that office unless it's life or death."

"My policy as well. This time I was summoned."

"Bad news?"

"Under normal circumstances it would be good news. In these times, not sure."

Charlie raised his hand holding his orders. "Just got orders of my rotation date, I'm first of October. That's only five weeks from now."

"Uh-oh. That will put pressure on Kim and you to wrap things up here. Wish I could trade with you. I'm first of February, I think."

Charlie said, "Hey, want a coffee? I'll buy, let's go where we can talk."

They picked up coffees from the office mess and headed to the privacy of the blueprint room. "The old man was in a good mood today so I thought I'd see if he'd agree to endorse papers getting Kim back to the States. Well, that will never happen. His hatred of the locals runs too deep. The bastard will never recommend approval of us getting married or spousal travel visa for Kim."

I said to him, "There must be other ways to do this, maybe the embassy can do something, or the Vietnamese authorities."

Chapter Twenty-seven

The Best of Times, the Worst of Times

The next few weeks, that is, the last of the month of July and the first weeks of August, I remember as the best of my time in Vietnam. The ARVN had succeeded, along with massive US Airforce and Navy airpower, in driving the NVA's Eastertide invasion back and out of South Vietnam. Charlie and I shared a feeling of pride in our counterparts, knowing they had received commendations for their efforts in defeating the North's daring offensive. For the time being we worried less about North Vietnam, but the Viet Minh guerrillas were still a danger in the South, especially at night.

Charlie and Kim had decided to marry and we spent many get-togethers celebrating that fact. There were discussions with Kim's family about Kim's future. By then the family that was so welcoming of Charlie had taken me in as an "adopted son." And so I participated in many discussions and dinners at their house on the farm. I was amazed at how open they were and how much the family knew about the US and the world. There were long debates in which we discussed the pros and cons of the Ceasefire Agreement and what it might mean for the South. My own scholarship left me crippled in the debates on racehorse attributes, but these few weeks became a wonderful time of sharing cultures and customs. The lessons we learned of the people and the land have lasted me a lifetime.

Kim's parents gave their blessings for the marriage. Though the family knew Kim's leaving would create a gap that would always be a source of sadness, her parents were resolute in agreement that it was her decision. But more than that, they were very fond of Charlie, and amidst the current turmoil and uncertainties they believed that for Kim's sake the marriage might be a blessing from above.

Deep down, most were beginning to believe South Vietnam would not be sustainable for long after the US pulled out. And pulling out looked more and more probable as the days went by. Binh himself had begun to explore contingencies for the family should the communists be victorious. Binh had some contacts in France, among them the Catholic priest in Paris with whom they corresponded at least annually. Binh had sent feelers to these people with Charlie's help via Navy FPO (of dubious legality) to scout for opportunities in France. As a war veteran fighting on the side of the French Union Forces (if only for a short time), he hoped to be looked upon as a preferred immigrant.

Charlie and Kim could have been married in a civil ceremony in Saigon, but a Catholic Mass at the basilica, which was Kim's preference, was out of the question due to timing. And since Captain Eagleton refused Kim's travel under Navy travel rules, the couple decided to delay for a proper marriage until they were in the States. Kim would have to travel to the US on a commercial ticket. For that, she'd need

Chapter Twenty-seven

a passport, which became the main obstacle. It was then that Margot volunteered to get into the act with her contacts in the Vietnam State Department and US Embassy.

Securing a passport in Vietnam was a notoriously slow process. But Margot liked a challenge. She vowed to push the application through the US and Vietnamese bureaucratic offices to make it happen in record time. Even with this effort, it would take a miracle to get it in time to allow Kim to travel on the same date as Charlie, which was October 1.

Late on the afternoon of August 15, Charlie was to meet Kim at Camille's apartment to go through a list of requirements needed for airline flights out of Saigon for The States. He was finishing up project work for the day when Margot dropped a package off on his desk. "This was received for you today, marked confidential from BUPERS (Bureau of Navy Personnel). You must be pretty darn important."

Charlie said, "Let's hope it's good news, although coming from BUPERS, it rarely is."

He ripped it open and began reading until he found the part he was dreading: *Due to readjustment in naval officer demands in RVN, your rotation date has been moved up to 1 Sept 1972.*

"Well, crap! Isn't that just dandy! Now my time left in Vietnam has been cut from six weeks to two weeks. I'm sure this is due to the accelerated withdrawal from Vietnam."

Not good news, but nevertheless Charlie was cool about it and decided there must be a way to handle it.

"How's it going with the passport, Margot?"

"Four to five weeks maybe; two weeks, ain't gonna' happen. It was submitted with all the documents only yesterday."

"Just do what you can, we'll have to look at Plan B. I'll talk to Kim tonight."

Charlie took a taxi to Camille's apartment in Cholon, handed the required piasters to the driver, and walked to Camille's front door. From around the corner he heard, "Hey! We're back here on the patio."

Kim hurried up to him happily excitedly and in her uninhibited way grabbed him tightly and planted a long hard kiss on his mouth in front of Camille. "Hello, husband to be! Ha!"

"Hi, Camille. What's *she* been drinking?"

"Rice wine on ice, actually," Camille said. "There's one for you on the table. We been drinking all afternoon, ha! Just kidding!"

They sat down and talked with Camille. Then Charlie broke the news of his orders. "I have good news and bad news. The good news is I am sitting here on a lovely patio drinking chilled rice wine from … " He looked at the bottle. "Vung Tau, with two of the most beautiful ladies in Saigon."

"Okay, Strickland, we know that. What's the bad news?"

"The bad news is I received new orders today. My rotation date has changed from October 1 to September 1. I must be on an airplane leaving Saigon on September the first. Two weeks from now."

Kim's reaction was normal. Cool, nonchalant.

"Whew!" she said. "We'll have to move quickly to get everything done. We can do it if we have to."

"That's what I thought; we will do it somehow. Margot says it will be near impossible to get your passport by then, so will need to go to some Plan B."

Kim said, "Before I forget, you and your buddy Joe are invited to our house tomorrow evening for a small dinner party. Mother is having

Chapter Twenty-seven

a little celebration for you and me. She's invited a few of my parents' friends. Camille is coming. Bao will have his friend Mi there, too. You can make it, right?"

"Sure, I'll talk to Joe when I get back tonight. We can talk about how you'll travel to the States, Plan B, with your parents, perhaps."

Charlie got back late that night after dinner with the two girls at a Chinese place in Cholon. He talked to me and that's when I told him they changed my orders, too. I was now to leave on September 15, two weeks after Charlie. The US Command was really beginning to accelerate the withdrawal of forces. I thought the party sounded like a good time; we decided to take the shipyard jeep, just the two of us.

Chapter Twenty-eight

Get-together at the Horse Farm

The next day, Charlie and I left the shipyard around 5 p.m. I left word with Margot where we were headed. Since it was just us Americans with no counterparts, we took a couple of extra precautions. We threw a PRC 25 field radio into the back of the jeep. We felt we should wear our tropical khakis since it was a party indoors but wore our Seabee combat boots underneath the dress trousers and carried our 45 pistols in case we needed to quickly travel by foot. Charlie knew Therese didn't like guns in the house, but we'd leave them in the coatrack as we went in.

After all these months, Charlie had worked out the shortest route, so he took the wheel. Charlie enjoyed driving out through this countryside with the big palms and the lush roadside vegetation. The sun had begun to wester and some beautiful peaceful flat clouds lay high and far in the west, but it would be hours before dark. Traffic was minimal and we arrived some twenty-five minutes later at the entrance to

Chapter Twenty-eight

Sun Stone Farm. Charlie made a mental note for the umpteenth time to ask Binh why he chose that particular name.

Normally, Charlie would park at the entrance and walk the trail to the house, but tonight we decided to drive the trail in case we stayed late or just as a general precaution. Some of the guests had arrived already and had chosen to park up by the barn as well.

Therese and Binh were beaming as we walked in and welcomed us like royalty. Charlie had by then become bold enough to embrace Therese, and he shook Binh's hand. Therese said, "So glad you could come tonight, Charlie and Lieutenant Joe. Oh! Two lieutenants! We must be important people!" They all laughed. "Please go in and meet the guests."

We walked into the house and hung the firearms in the coatrack. Charlie immediately saw Bao and Mi, who were talking to the police chief from Can An. The chief couldn't have been more welcoming to Charlie.

"Hello, Lieutenant, how are you and how is your friend Lieutenant Dao."

"Very good, very good on both accounts! Thank you. And you, Captain?"

"Quite well, thank you. Rebuilding of the police headquarters is going well. It needed updating anyway!"

He and Charlie chuckled about that. Charlie had done successful repair work on his relationship with the chief since the day of the mortar in Can An. Charlie had visited him once in the hospital where the chief was confined for three days. The chief knew he owed his life to him.

Charlie greeted Bao warmly and asked him about his history club meetings at the University. He was surprised that Bao was so forth-

Get-together at the Horse Farm

coming. He opened up and described one of the best discussions at the University yet over the Ceasefire Agreement.

Charlie said, "You and Mi have such a passion in that field. I'm glad you invited Mi tonight; his help was critical in Can An." He turned to Mi. "Good evening Mr. Mi, a pleasure to see you, sir."

Mi nodded to Charlie and me and said, "Yes, it's my pleasure." Nothing more, nothing less. What a poker face, never a trace or signal of recognition of knowing Charlie beyond a brief meeting at Can An many months ago.

Mi took a long drag on the same brand of cigarettes he smoked the night in the opium den, stared into his eyes, and never said a word. But during that eyeball-to-eyeball stare, did Charlie detect an ever-so-slight nod and a minimal curl of smile hidden mostly behind that cloud of smoke exhaled at that moment? Perhaps. That stare and the passage of secret knowledge between him and Charlie, understood only by them, was that together they had been successful. But never to be spoken of. Yet what a significant role he played in Charlie's life in Vietnam, and perhaps Charlie's entire life. More impactful than killing the boy with the sten. Certainly a close second to his meeting Kim. One had to admit saving the lives of one hundred-plus people from a bomb in a hotel could be counted as significant. They were partners in an accomplishment that could never be discussed, ever.

Kim and Camille were working in the kitchen. Kim heard Charlie's voice, turned, and her face lit up her bright eyes and big smile. Charlie returned the smile, and as he did he stepped back from the group and watched her come toward him. Still in her embroidered apron over a China blue ao dai, and along with her dark eyes and long flowing jet black hair, she was a beautiful young woman at the top of any scale.

Chapter Twenty-eight

As she came across the room in a kind of slow motion, he suddenly realized how much this party meant to her. With fourteen days left in Vietnam, this night could never be repeated. This was her engagement party, her wedding reception and her many impossible future visits with her family and friends, showing off potential grandchildren to grandparents. And how perhaps fifty years from now they would discuss together for the hundredth time what had happened this night, what everyone said and how they acted. What the ladies wore. What the gentlemen spoke about. What food she and Camille prepared and how delicious it was. How her father became misty-eyed when he gave the toast. What stories were told. They would laugh over the little secrets each had of others, and how they tried to act like they didn't think the others knew them. This was that night.

Kim came to Charlie and in her typical uninhibited way put her arms around him again and gave him a big hard kiss on the lips, took him by the hand, and raised her voice to all. "This is my friend Charlie Strickland from America, welcome to my family and friends!" This was followed by a big round of applause. At that point, Binh and Therese stepped up and presented Charlie with a gift of a beautiful leather briefcase they had purchased from the Duc Long leather goods shop in downtown Saigon. It was the most exclusive leather establishment in Saigon and also the place from which the finest racing saddles came. Charlie was overwhelmed by the gift, and Binh beamed at Charlie's appreciation.

The friends and family closest to Kim's parents were invited: Kim's Uncle Trung and Aunt Lan, as well as their best friends, Sang and his wife Anh of the Tuyen family. The Tuyen's land was next to Kim's family's, but they eventually changed their livelihood from agriculture and started a printing business in Saigon. The Tuyen family, as well as Binh's brother Trung and family, had come from North Vietnam during the migration in 1954. All came on the *US Montague*, and all were happy they made the decision nearly twenty years before.

They all wanted to make sure that Navy Lieutenant Charlie Strickland knew they came on an American Navy ship and that they served with American advisors to keep the South from communist rule. All of these families had a lot to lose if the North was victorious and wanted revenge.

Trung was Kim's favorite uncle. A jovial little man dressed in sporting clothes, round in shape, on military disability from fighting the Communists.

Charlie sought out Binh and Therese and discussed with them the issues of Kim's passport and the need to seek another way for her to leave. Binh asked the question, "Do you think Kim could get to the States via France?" Binh suggested he write to his friend, the Catholic priest in Paris, and ask for advice and possible help entering France if that became an option for Kim. "Flights may close down if an agreement is reached. We don't know what the rules will be." Charlie asked if Binh could write the letters soon. Charlie would mail them via the FPO (Fleet Post Office).

The party lasted longer than Charlie and I had thought, and we were glad we kept the jeep close by where we could see it. By the time we said our goodbyes, retrieved our firearms and drove back down the lane, it was 11 p.m. The trip back to Saigon was uneventful.

Chapter Twenty-nine

A Brutal Killing

A few days after the party on the twenty-fifth, Charlie was lying in his bed in his billet at 11 in the evening, absorbed in the John Le Carré novel, *The Spy Who Came in from the Cold*. The phone rang, and Charlie jumped up.

"Danged phone, rings once a month, always surprises..."

He picked up the phone: "Hello, Lieutenant Strickland speaking."

"Tiger, calling for Lieutenant Strickland, please."

Charlie thought, *Ha, there's Squeaky again.* His mood lightened. "This is Lieutenant Strickland … "

"Is this Lieutenant Strickland?"

"Yes, ma'am, this is he, Lieutenant Strickland speaking," trying to suppress a growing urge to laugh at this thus far ridiculous conversation."

"I have a call for Lieutenant Strickland, please hold for call … "

"Yes, thank you, I will do so."

After four or five minutes, a voice came on the line. "Hello, Charlie? It's Kim. I'm sorry to call so late, but I thought you should know." Her voice sounded shaky.

"Kim, what is it?"

"Charlie, I have terrible news."

"What news?"

"Bao's friend, Mi, he's been killed."

"What?! Mi? What happened?"

"He was taken we think by the Viet Minh, not sure. But they're saying Viet Minh. It was early this morning. It's terrible. He was tortured by whomever, before he was killed."

"No!"

"Yes, his body was dropped off at his parent's house, just after dark. They are devastated. Especially his father. There was a note left warning about passing information from one side to the other side. Father is really upset, too, especially because of the close friendship of Mi with Bao."

"Are you okay, Kim? What about Bao? Is he safe?"

"He's safe, but he's in shock. It was his best friend, you know. It's a terrible tragedy. Just horribly brutal."

"Did they come into his house? How did it happen?"

"I guess it was just before it got light out this morning. He had gone outside and was sitting on a bench … smoking. His mother didn't like him smoking in the house, Bao told me. They must have been waiting. His father said there were two guys. His father heard them struggling and went out. They were dragging him into a blue Fiat and took off a few seconds later."

"The bastards! How in hell can anyone be safe?"

He thought in silence for a few seconds. "You know, I decided long ago that Mi was one of the good guys. He was very smart, and he had a

Chapter Twenty-nine

heart that tried to do what was best for Vietnam's people. A tough one for Bao. Do they know who did this?"

"No, the police found the car, but it's just an old car that was stolen."

"Are you sure *you're* safe?"

"Oh, yes, there are police here and some soldier guys around. You know it's not that far that we live from their house. I must hang up now; it is costly to use this telephone, only emergency. Wanted you to know. So goodnight, Charlie."

"Goodnight, I will see you tomorrow somehow."

"I'll be at the track tomorrow."

"Okay. See you there. Be safe."

The next morning, Charlie took a taxi to COMNAVFORV (Commander Naval Forces Vietnam) in downtown Saigon. He entered a palatial white building and checked the office's map and tenant listings. Naval Intelligence was on the second floor. He took the stairs up, entered the suite of offices, and proceeded directly to the reception desk. "Would you please notify Commander Hargrove that Lieutenant Strickland is here to see him? From Naval Engineering Command at the Shipyard."

"Do you have an appointment?"

"No; no appointment."

"What is the nature of your business, Lieutenant?"

"Navy Intelligence."

"Can you be more specific than that, sir?"

"No, that's as specific as I'll get; he'll know what it concerns."

"Wait here, please, Lieutenant."

Charlie sat down and put his thoughts together about Mi, and what he needed to know before he left Vietnam. Two minutes later, Hargrove came out and said, "Hey, Charlie, follow me."

He was walking fast. "Let's go to the 'Quiet Room.'" He called over his shoulder, "Mindy, please bring us two coffees in number A down the hall ... both black."

"Yes sir, right away."

They entered A and Hargrove shut the door.

"Everything here today still SECRET, savvy?"

"Sure."

"I can guess why you're here: Mister Mi, correct?"

"Yes, sir, that's it. I guess you know by now he was *my* informant."

"Didn't, but do now. I got the news he was snatched early yesterday morning. They moved fast, took him to an interrogation cell over by the Parrot's Beak (an area near the Cambodian border where the border line between the two countries thrusts into Vietnam geographically in the shape of a parrot's beak). The cell was in a thick jungle area by the Cambodian border. It was the Viet Cong, the Viet Minh, without a doubt. It's how they work. We traced it quick with our Navy NIS guy up there. We found the car, we found the cell, but no dice. It was all over. We figure they hid his body all day back in the jungle. You probably know they dropped it off at his house late yesterday and left a note."

"Yes, I heard."

"It was a typical warning about what happens to informants. Wish we could have gotten there."

"Do you think it was related to his tip about the bomb at the Splendid Hotel?"

Mindy knocked to bring the coffee in; they stopped talking until she left.

Chapter Twenty-nine

"Could be, but I doubt it. None of the people we've been watching would be a likely suspect. I doubt if his former colleagues at the University would be that brutal. Mi was very discreet, but he didn't hide his allegiance to the South and local villages over there in his province. Someone ratted on him over there in that province, would be my guess."

"Do you think his friend Bao is in danger?"

"I can't answer that, Charlie. But Mi was more involved in the politics than Bao has shown to be. If he doesn't do something crazy, I doubt if these guys care much about him. If you ask me, Bao seems kind of oblivious to all this."

"Commander, do you think it's possible that the girl known as 'Tam' could be involved in this? Margot said the NIS had been watching her. I understand that she has disappeared and is no longer at the University. Nor does she come to the political meetings that Mi and Bao have been attending."

"It's possible. We still believe that she is an agent who provides information to the Viet Minh. But I doubt she is involved. I still think the information that triggered the incident came from the local province. Maybe even a connection to the provincial government."

Charlie said, "I just hope the killing of his friend doesn't somehow get Bao more involved."

"We may never know, especially at the speed we are leaving Vietnam now. When's your rotation date?"

"September first, sir, and I'll be out of here. Appreciate your time this morning, sir."

"You know, you can be proud of your service over here, Charlie, and the brave decision you made about the Splendid Hotel. It saved many lives. Good luck Charlie, and thanks for all your help."

"Thank you, sir." Charlie suddenly felt compelled to salute the commander; so he did. They shook hands and Charlie walked out.

Charlie took a taxi to the racetrack where Kim was talking to her dad and Bao. As he approached, he could see it was a family conversation; he didn't want to interfere so he waited on the bench by the Binh paddock. When they were finished, Binh and Bao waved to Charlie but went off together to bring some feed into the Binh's paddock.

Kim joined Charlie, took his hand with her two hands, looked up at him and said, "I can't believe they got Mi. I always thought highly of Mi and Bao is devastated. Father and I were discussing the whole thing with Bao. Such a…I think the term in the States is: 'a real wakeup call.'"

"That certainly is the correct phrase. I also thought Mi was an honorable man. He appeared to me as one who was smart enough and courageous enough to be part of the new generation needed to build the new Republic of Vietnam after the peace accords."

"That was Bao's passion, too. They made a good pair; both had so much interest in the history and politics of Vietnam."

"What's your father think?"

"He's worried about Bao's safety, even talked of Bao going somewhere for a while. His turn to train for the ARVN is coming up; perhaps he should speed the date up."

Chapter Thirty

Reviewing Options

It was the evening of August 30, and Charlie and Kim were at a shop in downtown Saigon getting copies made of Kim's birth certificate and other documents for the diplomatic visa Margot was researching. This was something that was possible in certain cases. They had finished with the copies and were tired and nervous.

It was coming down to D-Day, and no plan was in place for Kim to travel. Potential visas were being worked, but so far none had panned out. Charlie was also running out of time to finish a boat engine specs report that still needed dynamometer tests. If he didn't get the report finished, the engines would not be shipped from Guam after he left. He didn't want to leave them in the lurch. With the deadlines and no relief in sight for Kim to travel, Charlie was feeling testy.

"Charlie it's late," Kim said. "You're tired and need a break. We're hungry, let's stop to eat."

"All right, let's do pizza at the Palace. It's 6 p.m., shouldn't be crowded yet."

They walked up Hai Ba Trung and over to Tu Do. As they reached Tu Do, some enlisted army fellas out for drinking and carousing started walking behind them, and making comments. Charlie could see there were two of them. The bigger of the two said, "Where'd you pick up that piece, Navy boy?"

Charlie was irritated and getting more and more so, but he ignored the two until they got very vulgar and one said, "Hey, I think I'd like your date tonight, sailor boy." He grabbed Kim's hand and tried to pull her away.

Charlie pushed the big kid back and said, "Touch her again and you won't be able to walk home tonight, mister." Charlie's heart was pounding. The big fat brute was the one who had grabbed Kim, but the other was a smaller kid with doubtful strength. The brute outweighed Charlie by at least forty pounds but seemed a bit flabby and probably a little wobbly with all the cheap beer.

Walking farther toward the Palace, the big one wouldn't leave things alone. "Hey, sailor boy," he said, "you don't hear so well. I'm taking your cute little gook as mine tonight."

He grabbed Kim by the arm again and pulled hard. She jerked her arm free as Charlie turned to face the two. All the frustrations of the past week exploded, and he charged ferociously into the big brute. The big boy swung wildly at Charlie and missed, but Charlie landed a strong left fist deep into the brute's soft belly. The boy pitched forward and Charlie cut him down with a fast right across the left side of his head. He went down hard and lay there moaning. Charlie spun around quickly to address the smaller kid, who backed off immediately.

Chapter Thirty

Charlie was shaking and trying to catch his breath and said, "You see to your bud here, and get out of this area. I've got too much on my mind tonight to worry about the likes of you!" Charlie's heart was pounding, and he was breathing heavily. "Let's get our pizza, Kim."

Kim was breathing heavily, too, and said, "Well, I guess I better obey."

They were both still working on adrenalin, and that comment triggered a giddiness in both that transitioned into snickering. By the time they got to their table at the Palace they were into eye-watering belly laughter. Kim said while wiping her eyes, "Wow, I've seen a new side of you!"

Charlie's heart rate had slowed down a bit, and he said, "Sometimes I even surprise myself; first time for everything, but don't tell anybody!"

Another day had passed. It was August 31 and Charlie had given up trying to get Kim out of Vietnam with him on September 1. We met early at Kenny's for black market pancakes. It was around 6:30 a.m. when Kenny's opened. Josie came to our table right away and we ordered.

"Joe," Charlie told me, "I'm going to need your help this week after I've left."

I said I'd do anything I could, but said I was getting pretty short myself.

Charlie said with exasperation, "According to Margot, there's no chance of Kim's passport coming through today. She's trying to make it happen in the next couple of weeks while you're still here, but that's still a longshot. If the passport does come, it would be the least complicated solution. Just buy a ticket. I gave her the money."

Josie came with the stack of pancakes, and Charlie said to her, "Josie, I've got a quick question. What is the secret on these pancakes, I mean what if I wanted to make them like this myself?"

Josie leaned over and whispered in his ear, "Eggs and butter, double the amount the recipe calls for, especially butter; massive amounts of butter. And if you have enough, pure butter on the griddle, too."

"Really, that's all it takes?"

"That's it. A good source of butter. Eggs you can get easy right here. The trick is to cultivate a senior officer in the supply corps, feed him enough of these that he can't live without them. He'll gradually get a good reliable source of butter going and the supply side takes care of itself. Problem is, you get one trained, and he's gone in a year. So you've got to train one every year. I've trained several."

Josie winked and walked back to the kitchen.

"Okay, getting back to passports and such," Charlie said. "If the passport doesn't pan out, there are still two other paths we're working on. I'm just hoping one of these will come through. The first is: Margot and I have been working with the US Embassy to get a diplomatic visa for Kim through the State Department. We've already had the meetings and interviews, all the paperwork is submitted. Just waiting for the ruling, which should take about ten more days."

"The other path is something that Binh is working on with a Catholic priest in France. The priest is a personal friend of his and I understand the priest is attempting to acquire a type of French diplomatic visa. I don't understand exactly how it works. It should come through the FPO mail to our department or to Kim's family. Kim will contact you if it comes through to them. I'd sure appreciate it if you could keep an eyeball on these."

Chapter Thirty

"Of course I'll do that, it's no problem for me. Just remember I'm on that plane two weeks from tomorrow."

"Thanks, old buddy."

"Sure thing, now shut up and eat your pancakes. It'll be a long time before you get any more of these dogs."

I went back to the office, and Charlie did some small shopping of miscellaneous items he needed for the flight and some small gifts for his sister and aunt. He also bought a civilian shirt and trousers to wear home. Commander Hargrove had advised him not to wear his uniform on his flight home. "Best to avoid incidents between Vietnam protesters and returning service personnel at San Francisco International Airport, which have often been an issue on these flights."

Around noon, Charlie went back to his billet and packed his bags. He then went to the office to say goodbye to his team and the office people. It felt strange that he really had no real family to go back to, except Brigitte and his Aunt Sophie. The people he worked with and lived with here had been his family for the last nine months.

For their last night in Vietnam together, Charlie and Kim went to the Piccolo Restaurant on the wharf, which they thought was how they wanted to remember Vietnam. But it wasn't the kind of farewell evening they had hoped for. They didn't enjoy the food; they were too nervous to eat. The restaurant was noisy with a boisterous group of sailors at a big table next to theirs. It rained while they were in the restaurant and poured as they were leaving. Not a joyful affair.

Except they did talk seriously of the plans still in place to get Kim out of Vietnam. "You know, the three paths to get you out will be followed by Joe and Margot. If all three fail, then I'll come back and get you myself. It will take a while, I'll be mustered out of the Navy at Treasure Island in San Francisco Bay. I need to get us a place to live first, but hopefully you'll be there by then, anyway. I will attempt to contact you through the shipyard office here. Either Joe or Margot."

They left early and went to Camille's apartment. Where Kim stayed the night with Camille. That is where they said their real goodbye. Where they were more comfortable to say goodbye the way Kim wanted to.

"You'll never get me out of your mind after tonight, Strickland."

"Are you worried I won't come back for you?"

"Not after tonight."

Chapter Thirty-one

Goodbye Charlie

On September 1, I fired up the shipyard jeep and picked up Charlie at 8 a.m. We drove to the airport, passing the racetrack for the last time. "I wonder if I'll ever see that place again," Charlie said.

"Hard to say," I told him, "but I doubt it. I gotta believe one of these plans will work out. Remember, I'll be here two more weeks and just maybe Kim's regular passport will come through."

"Yeah, I hope. I want to get her out of here so bad. That business about Mi has really got Mi's family and Kim's family upset. You never know when those Cong bastards are going to strike or where. I wish to hell I could have gotten her out with me. You may have to help her get a ticket if that passport does come. I gave her plenty of money for that."

"That's a good boyfriend. I should really start calling you moneybags!"

"Hey, she doesn't know this, but back when she was ticked off at me and entered in that French Day Race with the big purse, I bet my monthly pay check on her to win that race."

"Whoa, kind of risky!" I said.

"Not really. There was only one other horse, the French filly, that could challenge Binh's black horse. It was obvious the other four wouldn't do much; they were older with mediocre records. The French hyped the filly so much, their big betting helped the odds for Black Martin. I saw that little French jockey showing off in front of the crowd on that flashy sorrel filly and I thought, *Why, that guy is going to screw up and try to show off in the race*. Which is exactly what he did. It's like I got two paychecks! Anyway, it'll help out getting a place to live when I get back."

"That reminds me, could you call me from the USO in about a week? Call me at Brigitte's number, Margot has it. Just to let me know what's going on. A week should give me enough time to get mustered out of the Navy and back to Brigitte's place near Columbus."

"Can do."

We drove in silence for five minutes, then I said, "You looking forward to getting out of the Navy?"

"Yeah, I am. I like the Navy, but I'm ready to get back into more of the engineering field. I may even go back to school."

They pulled into the main gate at Tan Son Nhut and Charlie said, "Just drop me at Camp Alpha; I think they make you do a drug test before you board."

I pulled the jeep up and jumped out as Charlie reached for his luggage behind us. I came around and said, "Looks like this is it, old buddy."

We did the man-hug thing, and Charlie said, "Yeah, looks like. We gotta keep in touch, Joe."

Chapter Thirty-one

"We will, things will work out over here; you be safe."

"So long, old buddy."

Charlie grabbed his bags, turned around with a big smile, and said, "Go Bucks!"

"Oh, yeah!"

Charlie entered Camp Alpha and was gone. I climbed into the jeep and headed back to Saigon.

Chapter Thirty-two

Eliminating Options

I stopped by at the track later that morning on my way back to the airport where I had to retrieve an air freight package of parts for an electrical transformer. Danh and I were going down to help an outpost near Binh Thuy install a larger generator to improve base power. We were still trying to finish a number of projects, though I had less than two weeks left in Vietnam. Kim was exercising the chestnut, cantering the horse at a steady speed around the one and a quarter mile track.

When she came round, she stopped and said, "Hi, Joe."
"How many times do you take her around like that?" I asked.
"Guess."
"No idea, maybe two times?"
"Four."
"Seems a lot. Why that's five miles."

Chapter Thirty-two

"Oh, this little girl can go twice that distance easy enough. We're not going very fast. She's not very good on the track yet; she needs to get more used to it so we go for longer time and slower speed." Short pause. "I take it you got Charlie off this morning?"

"Yes, everything went okay; he's on his way by now. Next time you see Charlie, he'll be out of the Navy."

"Yes, next time I see him, everything will be different."

"Kim, I'm here to help in any way I can in getting your travel arrangements worked out. Charlie explained where everything stands. But I'm leaving also in two weeks from today, so I'm hopeful we can get it done before then!"

"You're a good guy, Joe. You're a good buddy to Charlie."

"Thanks."

He paused and looked around the track. "Well, I've got to go for now. Danh and I are heading to Binh Thuy to finish a project there, so … see you soon. Contact me anytime, call Margot, she will get hold of me."

"Be safe, Joe."

Five more days went by and there was no news of any kind on the three back-up plans to get Kim out. Two more days and I was supposed to call Charlie at Brigitte's place. I wanted to have some good news to tell Charlie when I called. When I got to the office that morning, Margot was waiting for me.

"Any news from Kim on the Paris connection?"

"Nope, nothing," I told her. "I hope we get something today. Charlie said they would send any correspondence to our FPO address. Maybe today."

"Bummer," Margot said. "I spent two hours at the Vietnamese State Department yesterday. I tried to cash in every favor I had over there, but no dice. They're consumed with planning their own exits. Confidence in the government is really starting to fade. They're very polite and all. They say they'll make sure to 'Process Urgent,' but that doesn't mean squat. Kim's paperwork hasn't even been reviewed. I'm convinced her passport won't make it. Honestly, I think we have a better chance with the diplomatic passport at the embassy. I'm going over there today to see how it's going."

"Dammit! Something has to break through here real quick, or we'll be up that certain creek."

"I almost hate to tell you this, Joe."

"What?"

"I just got my orders to leave. I'm on a plane the day after you."

"No!"

"Yeah, unfortunately. It's the Peace Accords thing."

"It is what it is."

I couldn't get through to Charlie on the eighth at the USO, but I did on the ninth. He made it to Brigitte's place in Ohio. He said he was out of the Navy, a civilian again. I brought him up to speed. Kim's regular passport probably won't get through in time, I said, but we still had the diplomatic visa in process and presumably Paris. At that point we lost the line and couldn't reconnect. Pretty much of a downer phone call; he sounded depressed.

Later that day, I stopped by the track and brought Kim up to date. She was polite and thanked me, but the situation was beginning to wear on her.

Margot cornered me early morning on September 10. Over coffee in the mess room, she relayed the conclusions of her latest meeting

Chapter Thirty-two

with the American Embassy. "The only way to get the diplomatic visa through was by a top level endorsement from a flag rank or minimum of captain rank. They added that if the particular unit's captain were to sign off, such as Eagleton, it would most likely be granted. Not guaranteed, but 'most likely.'" Deep breath. "I don't know any admirals, do you?"

I told her we would have to go back to Eagleton and try one more time.

She agreed. "If we don't try, we may as well scratch this option now."

I suggested we needed a good plan before we went in there this time.

"Yes," Margot said.

I suggested meeting with the captain the next day, first thing.

"I have an idea," Margot said. "I don't know anything about the captain's life outside the office. Not even where he lives. I have less than one week left in this country, and I'm getting bolder by the day. I'm thinking of following him after work to see at least where he lives. He is very secretive. Maybe I'll learn something that will help us in getting him to sign that visa."

I told Margot she *was* getting bold and asked if she wanted some company on her excursion.

She answered, "Of course. I'd love some company."

Margot had a taxi waiting out of sight. The captain locked his door and left the office at precisely 6 p.m. By the time he got to the parking lot, his taxi rolled in and he climbed in the rear seat.

Margot and I scrambled to get out of the office and down the street and into our taxi before the captain was out of sight down Thong Nhut Street. We followed him at a distance in heavy traffic, nearly losing him twice. We drove a good twenty minutes and finally into a quiet, nice looking neighborhood. The captain emerged from the taxi and entered a well-guarded senior officer BOQ on the south side of downtown.

We pulled over into street parking and said to each other, "Well, this is boring."

"Let's wait a few minutes," Margo said.

We sat in the car fifteen minutes and were about to leave when a man in a dark jacket, khakis, and ball cap came out of the building just as another taxi pulled up. The man, carrying a packet the size of small briefcase, looked quickly around then got into the car.

"That's him," Margo said. "Follow that taxi, sir."

The taxi headed back to downtown, then along the river, and turned toward Cholon. We drove another ten minutes and went deeper and deeper into the bowels of that crowded mass of humanity.

Margot said quietly, "You have your Navy .45, right?"

I answered affirmatively, then said in jest, "I'll protect you, don't worry."

"Won't be necessary," she said. She pulled up her light sweater and revealed a 9 mm NIS issue in a Velcro holster taped to her bare midriff.

I looked at her askance and said, "Who the hell are you, Margot?"

She looked over at me with a little smile and said, "It's a secret."

"Sometime tell me that secret, but not now."

The captain's taxi had stopped to wait for pedestrians crossing the street, then turned right down a small alley named Chin Yu. He stopped halfway to the next block, then pulled forward very close to the building so that no one could enter from the driver's side. The captain got out and walked a hundred feet up the street and down some steps that went to a below ground apartment.

Our taxi stopped a ways back from the captain's. The alley was quite narrow and the two taxis were the only vehicles in it. We were

Chapter Thirty-two

concerned the captain's taxi driver or the captain himself would become suspicious if we parked and started snooping around the apartment. Suddenly his taxi took off, evidently waiting until the captain was safely inside. Presumably the taxi would return later to retrieve him.

This was our chance. We exited the car. The taxi did not want to wait and said, "Too dangerous to sit here."

Margot pulled out a two hundred-piaster note and said, "Nam phut, monsieur (*five minutes, sir*)."

He nodded acceptance, and Margot handed him the note.

We hurried up to the apartment. Standing behind a sewer pipe coming down flat against the building exterior, we peered into an opened curtained window. Looking downward we could see the captain sitting and talking with an attractive looking Vietnamese woman in her early twenties. She was dressed respectfully and on her lap sat the packet he had carried in.

One could see it was a thick packet containing a bundle of piaster notes. Suddenly we saw an infant of three or four months old in a modern car seat on the ground at their feet. The little one was smiling up at the couple in a scene out of a Hallmark movie. All seemed to be in good spirits in the modestly appointed apartment. Our five minutes were up, Margot pointed to the car, and we hurried back. The taxi headed back and I suggested we stop at Kenny's and discuss what we'd witnessed. Plus, I was starved.

We sat down to a couple of beers and burgers. Margot asked me what I witnessed. I told her that visually, it could have been a father with his daughter and his first grandson but it was probably more like a man at the end of his long Navy career trying to make amends for one horrible drunken night the previous year.

Margot said, "My sentiments exactly. Nothing I expected. We all have our secrets, don't we? It could be the reason he extended his tour over here this time last year. I could never understand why he did that. It was obvious he hated everything about Vietnam."

"We all have our weaknesses," I said, "and yet I can't help thinking of him in a different way now. I kind of wish I hadn't seen that tonight. I'm sure he's painfully conflicted, especially knowing that we Americans are and will continue to be leaving. Now I believe we must be very careful in how we approach the subject of the visa tomorrow."

"Yes, Joe, we must respect that it's an ethical question. I need to think more tonight. We're on the schedule to meet with the captain at 8 a.m. Let's meet at 7:30 for coffee."

We grabbed a taxi, dropped Margot at her apartment, and I headed back to my BOQ on Hai Ba Trung.

At 7:15 a.m., Margot and I sipped bad coffee and agreed not to bring up what we'd seen the prior evening in our little meeting that morning with Eagleton. There were too many lives at risk to be ruined in taking that tack; the captain's long career (of which we knew nothing, good or bad), his wife, his family, the young girl, and the little one. Perhaps he had a plan for them. We agreed to concentrate on Charlie's positive engineering and advising accomplishments in Vietnam and the upstanding lady that Charlie has chosen in Nguyen Kim Li, and the unusual circumstances of timing involved in pulling out of an eleven-year war to meet an election goal.

I told Margot, "I'm in agreement with this plan, but I must say, on the question of ethics, you have a larger heart than I. It still bothers me that Eagleton appears to be the ultimate hypocrite. If I'm honest with myself, I have to say it's not all my heart that's talking, but the fact that

Chapter Thirty-two

neither Charlie nor Kim would ever condone us using what we saw last night to force a signature. It would dishonor them."

We took a last swig of the horrible coffee and headed down the hallway to the captain's office. It was a congenial, friendly meeting until we got down to brass tacks. We laid out our case beautifully, even mentioning the embassy's statement that the captain's signature carried such weight that (little bit of a literary license here) it would in all probability ensure that the visa was issued.

The captain sat and stared at us for an interminable amount of time. There was a terribly uncomfortable silence in the room. My dander rose with each second.

I made up my mind to stare back at him for as long as it took. Didn't seem to bother him; he seemed inhuman. Finally, he said, "You people still don't understand. These people are incompetent. With all the billions we've poured into this little patch of Third World shanty towns, they are still losing this war, and disgracing our great country. These people are not like you and I. They are inferior, they can't fight, they won't fight. They have their own inferior culture, twelfth-century agriculture, tasteless and stinking food. I would never, ever, be the source of approval for allowing one of these gooks into our country. You may be excused."

Margot picked up the paperwork and started to leave the room. I sat in my chair and stared at the captain. I was so angry at the last burst of slurs that I was shaking and felt like strangling the bastard. But I calmly said, "Sir, may I ask you a question, sir?" Margot looked at me and did a slight headshake. The captain said nothing, one way or the other. Margot put her hand on my arm and said, "Come on Joe, we have work to do."

We walked out together; it was the last time I ever talked to the man.

It was only 9 a.m. "I'm going to Kenny's," I said to Margot. "I'm having pancakes. Coming?"

"Of course, I'm coming."

We went to Kenny's and had black market pancakes and a little better coffee. The meeting was such a disaster neither of us wanted to talk about it. We talked of other options for Kim. Short of Charlie coming back and staying here for what could be months, the only possibility left was the French priest. As far as I knew, no one had heard anything since the correspondence was mailed to him from our FPO address.

The next day was September 12, about the last day to receive any type of documents from the French to process and line up tickets for flight by the fourteenth. My flight was on the fifteenth, and I wanted to get Kim out a day before that. It was all last minute, and the stress was building.

Chapter Thirty-three

Goodbye Kim

I got up on the twelfth and spent the whole morning tying up loose ends on the projects with Danh. He and I grabbed a sandwich at 11:30 a.m. and I went to a small get-together in the shop to say goodbye to the team. The mail came at around 1 p.m., so I wanted to be back in the office by 1:30. I made it back by 1:45. No Margot. I asked where she was and found her lunching with the Vietnamese secretaries on the picnic table outside the office.

"Did you get it?" she said.

"Get what?" I asked.

"The French package, the damn French package; it's on your desk covered with PAR AVION stamps and stickers."

I went to my desk, found it, ripped it open, and was astonished. It contained an official French-Vietnam Visa signed by a French state department official. With copies authorized by the Vietnamese Embassy,

France, and a raft of instructions in French that I would need translated. The package also contained a personal letter to Binh from his priest friend, Father Desjardins.

"Holy shit!" I blurted.

I couldn't have been higher. I ran outside, grabbed Margot by the shoulders, and planted a big kiss on her lips despite the mayonnaise left from the ham sandwich she'd just finished. She took a big breath and came back on me with an even meaner lip lock. I indulged her. I gave her a hug and hoped I didn't feel a 9mm taped to her midriff. Probably the biggest display of public affection she had had since arriving in Vietnam eighteen months ago.

The two Vietnamese secretaries lunching with her were bent over and choking with embarrassed laughter.

I went to the track and found Kim with her father, showing them the documents and explained the best I could. Kim was elated. I handed Binh the personal letter from the priest. He stared at it for a long time, then said he would open it later. Kim and I agreed to meet early next day at the track. We would visit the French embassy and take care of all communications necessary with France, obtain all documents as needed, and work out the tickets.

Kim said she still wanted to leave on the fourteenth, if possible. Her father wasn't happy that all of this was decided so close to her flight date.

"Oh! So quickly, so quickly."

It left her with only two days to get everything done. I advised Kim that this meant she must have everything ready by the following evening. We would try to make the flight as late as possible but Air France and most other westbound flights left in the morning.

I told Kim that if there were people she needed to see or personal items to take care of, this would be the time.

Chapter Thirty-three

She looked at me earnestly and said, "Oh Joe, I understand all that. I am already packed and have my valuables stowed. I've said my goodbyes to everyone except closest family. Don't worry, Joe; my mind was made up months ago, in spite of the possibility of never returning."

I told her I knew she would be and that I'd see her tomorrow morning at the track.

Kim returned home and spent most of the afternoon with her mother. At 4 p.m. she walked down to the stable. Kim loved the feel and the smell of the horse stable. It was cool and dark with a comfortable safe feeling. The hard packed dirt floor, the smell of the big muscular animals themselves, along with the grains and fresh bromegrass hay mingled with aromas of liniments and rubbing compounds produced a distinct essence. It conjured up images and feelings of horse racing, the people involved and special horses. She knew this was part of her life she would miss terribly.

As she came into the stable, Black Martin pricked his ears forward and moved to her. She reached up and scratched his neck and said, "Come on, fella, we're going for a walk."

Kim bridled him and walked him down the lane slowly to admire and remember the best horse she had ever raced. When she got to the end of the lane she pulled him over to the stone bench at the entry way, stepped up and mounted the big gelding. They entered the roadway and she put him into an easy trot down to the little bridge that crossed the small canal near their home. She walked him from the road down a small embankment to a trail that followed the canal. Kim walked the horse along the canal and watched the canal traffic pass slowly by.

The passersby were spaced out in the narrow canal. Some were families with kids and the smells of food cooking on gas burners wafted across her path like invisible spirits offering prayers and blessings of good fortune. Some were fishermen going home with their catch for the day. A boy motored slowly by with his small sampan filled with two heavy oval-shaped baskets of Ben Luc pineapples that radiated in the sun. It brought to mind the sweetest taste of Asia. Kim returned a friendly wave to the boy.

She stopped the horse. He stood with noble head held high and ears pricked forward looking across the canal to the flat delta paddies. She turned her face into the light breeze and breathed in all she could of the sights, sounds, and smells of the place where she was born and had lived for twenty years.

She swung the big horse around and said, "Okay, Mr. Black Martin, enough of this sentimentality. I've got a new race I have to run starting tomorrow, and you can't be any part of this one."

He trotted back along the canal and up to the road. Then she cantered back down the road to the entrance of Sun Stone Horse Farm and put him into a gallop down the lane for the last time.

Next morning I picked up Kim early, and we headed to the French Embassy. They were very efficient, as I remember. Their officers were well acquainted with the procedure, due to the sizeable population of French who still tarried in Saigon. When the documents were translated we found Kim's ticket was paid for by an anonymous donor and that Father Desjardins would meet her airplane upon her arrival in Paris. We also learned the embassy could make the flight arrangements from their office, even to the extent of issuing Kim's ticket, a big timesaver for us that morning. The only flight left for Europe on the fourteenth had a boarding time of 10:15 a.m. Saigon time.

Chapter Thirty-three

When the ticket was issued, Kim held it in her hand and admired it. In those days the ticket was tucked inside a prestigious white envelope emblazoned with the tricolor logo and an image of an Air France aircraft. Kim looked as though she held a million dollars in her hand.

"Quite exciting," she said. "I've never flown before!"

I was so relieved to see that ticket in her hand. It had been a trying two weeks since Charlie left. She put the documents and tickets safely away in her handbag. On the way out, we stopped in the lobby for a cup of tea and to go over any remaining items she needed.

"So you'll get to Paris, and Father Desjardins will meet you, and you'll have a place to stay. It will be easy to call Charlie from Paris. The telephone service is very good there. How will you get to the US?"

Kim said, "I was thinking about that last night. Maybe there could be an opportunity to get married in Paris. Charlie could come and meet me in Paris. And maybe we could get married at Sacre-Coeur on Montmartre! And then I'll be an American's wife. I may be able to get a visa as Charlie's wife. We will figure it out."

I told her that sounded good to me. "Think big!" I said.

We grabbed a taxi; I took her back to the track to be with her parents her last day. I told her I'd meet her at the airport the next day no later than 8 a.m. Then I headed back to the BOQ to get packed myself.

She was there with her family early the next morning. A happy yet sad day. I helped to see her through passport control, customs, and baggage check. She got her boarding card and was ready to go with about forty-five minutes to spare. There was plenty of time for final private words with her family. But it was a sad and stressful time for all. There was no way it could have been different. Parting under the shadow of a probable regime change and sending a daughter into the world alone to find her way to America would never be easy.

The family embraced and shared final words and kisses, a desperate day for all concerned but one with a degree of hope. I walked her to the steel gate on the tarmac which was guarded on each side by US Military Police. The MPs were still in control of security at the large Tan Son Nhut Air Base, not yet turned over to Vietnamese authorities. A new widebody Air France 747-100 stood waiting. Kim showed her precious Air France boarding card to the soldiers.

She hugged me quickly and said, "Goodbye, Joe, thanks for everything. I'll never forget your kindness."

She turned and waved one last goodbye to her family, knowing full well as did they, it might be for the last time. She walked bravely across the tarmac and up the long moveable stairs to meet a smiling and welcoming French stewardess. She stopped and from the height of the platform looked around at the countryside of her birth, then entered the cabin and was gone.

I never heard from or saw any of Binh's family after that. I went directly to the USO and called Charlie. I gave him all the details of her flight and her contacts in Paris and wished the best to both of them.

Part Two

Chapter One

San Francisco, Spring, 1991

In the spring of 1991, Vietnam seemed a distant past. After all, nearly twenty years had gone by since I was traipsing around the Mekong Delta with my old counterpart Danh. I wondered about Danh sometimes and where he ended up. Vietnam was not the same. It was beginning to change rapidly now, and becoming more westernized.

Charlie and I hadn't done a very good job of keeping in contact with each other. For the first few years we were faithful with phone calls, cards, and some letters. We talked in 1975 when only two and a half years after the ceasefire, North Vietnam ignored the agreement, overwhelmed the South militarily, and took over the country. We discussed what may have happened to the people we knew. There was no word about Kim's parents. Communications to or from inside the country were closed down. None of the possibilities for the people we knew seemed positive. My life and Charlie's took different directions and gradually we drifted out of contact.

Chapter One

I had gone into aerospace engineering and for the last nineteen years I had worked for a large US technical company that was getting into robotics. I found myself in May of that year on a business trip to Seattle with a layover in San Francisco. When I arrived at SFO International late that morning, I had forgotten I had five hours before connecting to my PSA jet up to Seattle. I realized it was time enough to visit the city for a couple of hours, instead of sitting in a bar or browsing the airport shops. After all, just before Vietnam I'd spent several months living in Vallejo just up the road.

I was stationed at Mare Island Training Center up there and spent lots of time hiking around the city of San Francisco during those months. It was the time of the hippies and the flower children and all the music that went with it. Would any of the old haunts still be there? I put my briefcase in a self-lock and exited the terminal. A beautiful spring day waited for me. I jumped on a city shuttle bus that made the rounds every thirty minutes for the ride to the city and back.

At 11 a.m., I stepped off the bus at Taylor and O'Farrell streets. I walked a block toward Union Square where I took a cable car down to Fisherman's Wharf. I felt like a good walk, so with my map I took off for a look around and a place to grab a sandwich. I walked past the Wax Museum, just as earthy as ever. I tried to find Cost Plus but couldn't. I thought it might be the big box store now sitting where I thought Cost Plus used to be. Time passed quickly in a city with fascinating sites on every block. I was getting hungry and realized the time zones were the cause. I began a search for food. Tarantino's Restaurant was still there right on the water, but that was too fancy.

I vaguely remembered an Irish coffeehouse somewhere up Powell Street and headed there. *Bingo!* Found it in five minutes and not overly crowded. It was after the main lunch crowd. I walked in and sat down.

San Francisco, Spring, 1991

Put my jacket on a chair and unfolded the map in front of me while I waited for a menu.

I recognized him immediately, standing at the bar. Kind of had his back turned to me, but I could see the side of his face. Tall, young-ish looking man in his forties, in a herringbone sport coat, newspaper under one arm, Irish coffee in the other, talking to the bartender. I should say laughing with the bartender or maybe howling is a better word, as if one of them had just blurted out the punch line of a very creative joke. There was no mistaking that voice or laugh.

He was no more than twenty feet from me. I called out to him, "Always laugh at your own jokes, Mister?"

Charlie stopped and stood still looking straight ahead for a couple of seconds. You could tell he was mulling the familiar voice. Then said without moving, "What the devil! I don't believe it!"

He turned and saw me and said "I still don't believe it! Joe Savage!"

We shook hands vigorously and I said, "Long time passing since Vietnam."

"Yes, it has been."

"What are you doing here?" we both said. I told him about my layover on the way to Seattle."

Charlie said, "I'm here in Frisco at an incredibly boring CAD design symposium from the college. I'll be here a couple of more days. What time's your connecting flight?"

"I've got an hour before I catch that shuttle back. Is Kim here with you?"

"No, she's home with our daughter."

"How is she, Charlie? Jeez, it's been so long since I've seen you guys."

"She's fine, we're all doing fine."

Chapter One

Charlie sat down and we ordered a couple of sandwiches and beers. I said, "It's been a long time since beers at Kenny's. Ever hear from Kenny? Wonder if he got out."

"Oh, Kenny and his wife got out. If anybody got out it was Kenny." I had to laugh at how much faith he had in old Kenny.

We used up the hour sharing all the information of our lives that we could. He said, "You're in New Jersey, not that far from us in New York State. We have a small farm. It would be great if you could come on up to our place, stay the weekend. I'm sure Kim would love it."

I had to catch the shuttle and Charlie had to get back to the symposium, so we parted around 2:30 and promised each other we'd get together soon. Maybe this summer? At least we would try.

Chapter Two

Visit to Ithaca, Autumn, 1991

It was a Friday afternoon, and I had just finished a late lunch at Arlie's in Flora Park, New Jersey. My consulting office was only a block away. I had left the cozy corporate world and started my own consulting firm.

I stepped out of the restaurant and took a minute to enjoy the beautiful warm Indian summer day. Some of the early New England leaves were turning. As I strolled back to the office, I began to think that I really had nothing that was pressing and no travel plans scheduled the next few days. This might be a good weekend to take Charlie up on the invite to his farm in New York State.

I closed the office, went home, and on the spur of the moment I called Charlie. Kim answered, and I said, "Is that you?"

"Of course it's me," she said.

She answered as though the twenty years was twenty minutes. She summed up: no plans for the weekend, delighted to have you, you must

Chapter Two

stay overnight Saturday. I was overjoyed. I packed an overnight bag and spent the rest of the afternoon checking out the old '53 MGTD roadster for roadworthiness. I'd had it overhauled recently and was itching for a weekend trip to see how the old girl ran.

I started out early next morning. It was a perfect day for driving, sunny and crisp. I took local roads first to test the car, passed through Parsippany, and at Bloomingdale picked up US 287/87 North and was soon in New York State. I turned left at Route 17 and took the two-lane west across New York State. By the time I reached Binghamton it was midafternoon and I stopped for a break. The MG was running fine. I topped off the tank, grabbed a coffee, and motored on.

I took the Ithaca exit and journeyed north. Soon I was travelling in beautiful rolling countryside. I had forgotten how much agriculture and sweet farm country was still alive and well in rural New York State. It made me feel good about taking the weekend off. My map said I had another thirty-five minutes to reach the Strickland place, just outside a town called West Linford.

I saw a sign for Cornell University and within minutes I was motoring on a small backroad of rolling meadows and woodlands. I recognized the Strickland farm property a quarter mile before I reached their driveway. Adjacent to the road ran a white board fence that enclosed a pastureland. I pulled the car over to take in the beautiful setting and maybe prepare myself mentally for meeting Kim, who I hadn't seen since the last days in Vietnam almost twenty years ago.

It took me back to a desperate day for her whole family when she was facing a do or die life event that seemed nearly out of control. I tried to remember that day with Kim and her family and what a major life event it was for all concerned. I thought about how this was just one event in thousands of major life events that were precipitated by the Vietnam War.

Presently, I saw a teenage girl in black riding boots cantering a big black gelding along the board fence coming toward me. I could see a long dark ponytail swinging side-to-side and an eager smile on the face under the helmet. She pulled the big animal up as she approached and walked him to the fence.

"Betcha I know who you are! Dad's Vietnam friend, right?"

"You are so right," I said. "My name's Joe. Nice horse; you ride well!"

"Thanks, I ride okay; my mom rides better. She's the best in the family; she used to race horses on a racetrack."

"I believe you. What's your horse's name?"

"Black Martin. Mine's Therese."

"Nice names, I've heard them before."

"Yeah, not too original."

She looked at the car. "I like your car! My parents are dying to see you, come on up to the house."

I turned into a long gravel driveway lined with mature sugar maples, both sides. A colonial house of quarried limestone was set dead center at the end of the hundred-yard drive, behind a circular pavement that surrounded an English type garden of Bonsai and other Asian plantings. Large hardwoods provided shade around the house and frontal area.

Charlie and Kim were waiting at the front entrance when I drove up, and they hurried out to meet me as I approached.

"Welcome to the Strickland homestead, old boy," Charlie called.

I called back, "Ha! Well, good to be at the Strickland homestead, old boy!" Laughter all around.

Chapter Two

Hugs to Charlie and Kim in turn. "Long time passing since Saigon. So wonderful to see you guys…beautiful place you have here."

Kim said, "And here is Therese, our high school senior, heading to college next year."

Therese was a mirror image of Kim.

"Ohio State, I hope," I said.

"Nope, Cornell for me…if I get accepted."

Charlie said, "She'll make it, a hard worker, and good grades. Plus she's worked on campus and her parents both teach at Cornell! Me, engineering, and Kim, art department. Come on in and meet Brigitte. She's living with us now. You remember my younger sister."

Brigitte met them coming in. "Of course I remember Brigitte! How could I forget the high school girl you sneaked up to our dorm room at Ohio State! Got us into all kinds of trouble."

"You guys were crazy then," Brigitte said through a big hug. I was surprised at her youthful and fit appearance. "Wow, still got that old MG?" Brigitte continued to be the pleasant outgoing lady I remembered from years ago. She seemed to enjoy kidding Charlie.

"Hey, you should have kept *your* TR-3, Brother Strickland!" She referred to Charlie as Brother, even to that term of endearment, *Brother Strickland*.

"I've always called him that, long as I can remember," she said. The strong sibling bond was pleasant to observe.

The house was a virtual art museum from Kim's work. We talked about old times and caught up on current lives. Finally Kim said, "We found out my father died yesterday; he had a long life but missed Mom greatly since she passed away two years ago."

I offered my condolences and that my memories were of a wonderful man.

Charlie said, "We'll be flying over for the funeral this coming week… all three of us. Actually, we're leaving on Tuesday."

That evening, we went to a wonderful Italian restaurant called Isabella's. We talked about the Binh family history and how there was hope for the future in Vietnam. I learned that two years after we left Vietnam, Kim's brother, Bao, married the young lady named Tam. I was happy to hear it. I thought it was a good match. Both shared a common passion for government. They had a daughter that must have been about thirteen or fourteen years old by now. Bao and Tam both worked for the new government. Kim wasn't sure what they were doing.

We retired to their home for a nightcap.

"Brandy, Joe?"

"Yes, but one finger only for me."

Brigitte and Therese had wandered to their rooms after their 'good nights.' The three of us sat in the den and sipped our brandies and mused about how the world had changed.

"The last time I saw you, Kim," I said, "you stood on a tall platform ready to walk into that airplane. What was it like? What happened after that morning? Did the priest meet you in Paris? I left the next morning and never saw or heard from your family after that."

"Oh, it was a long day, Joe, and very sad that morning but also exciting. Yes, we landed as planned at Charles De Gaulle Airport in early afternoon. It was raining in Paris. I didn't care! The airport was huge, intimidating. I had that special visa; at first they didn't know how to handle it. Passport control pulled me out of line, but then found my name; it was all legal and I was cleared after a few questions. Father Desjardins was at baggage claim. Super nice man. Of course he wanted to know all about the family.

"Did you stay at the rectory?"

"No, he had me set up in a small place in the Saint-Germain-des-Prés area called L'Hotel Saint-Sulpice, a mom-and-pop hotel. The couple that ran it were very helpful. When Charlie came over we stayed there the whole time, two months! Can you believe it?! We still trade Christmas cards with that couple.

"I called Charlie that first night, from my room. Back then it was unbelievable that I could do that so easily. I tried but couldn't get through to my parents. I sat down and wrote them a long letter from my room. I remember when I retired for the night, I couldn't believe I was sleeping in a hotel in Paris, France.

"I arrived four days later," Charlie said.

"Yes," Kim added. "We were married at Saint-Sulpice Church. Close by to the hotel. Father Desjardins organized it. He gave me away. He showed me the long letter that my father had sent him that explained the whole situation."

"Must have been the letter he'd given me to mail through the FPO," Charlie said.

"So, two-month honeymoon in Paris, must be nice!" I said to them both.

Kim said, "It *was* nice," as she smiled at Charlie. "It was perfect."

"Actually, it took nearly two months to get the visa and approvals for Kim to fly back with me."

It was getting late, and we were all starting to fade. I told them I was ready to hit the sack. "Thanks for a wonderful visit and be safe on your big trip. I'll plan to leave tomorrow first thing."

Early next morning I climbed into the MG and headed back to New Jersey—after they agreed to ship me back some of my favorite pineapples from Ben Luc.

Chapter Three

Return to Vietnam, Autumn, 1991

The Boeing 747-300 lined up several miles out over the South China Sea, with a watery sun rising behind it. The captain called for seat belts to be fastened, and the big bird began to float down toward Ho Chi Minh City, Peoples Democratic Republic of Vietnam.

The Strickland family arrived at Tan Son Nhut Airport, Vietnam, at 8:15 a.m. local time, in a steady drizzle. It was hot and sticky. They were tired after the long nighttime flight and suffering from jet lag. Charlie's mind went back in time as he recognized the sights, sounds, and smells of Asia that greeted him the first time he stepped down on this tarmac many years before. The chattering sing-song language, ladies strolling in ao dai dresses, a whiff of nuoc mam fish sauce. Steam rose from the pavement as they walked to the terminal to baggage claim.

Kim's eyes lit up as she saw her brother, Bao, there to meet her as planned. She picked him out of the crowd at once and felt a sense of

Chapter Three

joy as she saw him still the tall youngish good looking big brother she remembered. Kim and Bao embraced for a long time and traded private words of condolences for their father.

She introduced Uncle Bao to Therese who remarked on the similarity in appearance of brother and sister. Charlie and Bao shared a good-natured handshake. There was ample room in Bao's new Jeep Cherokee SUV for the three travelers and their luggage, which Bao stowed neatly in the luggage compartment. Bao was plainly excited for this reunion and said, "Tam and our daughter, Lia, are at home anxious to see everyone. Too tight in the car to bring them."

Driving to the city they passed the old Phu Tho Racetrack, which had been shut down after the communist regime took over in 1975. The grounds had been turned into a sort of sports complex, with soccer fields, golf courses, and walking tracks. But the old one-and-a-quarter mile track remained. New construction on the infield was going on, which appeared to be modern housing units.

Young Therese viewed the area with awe. "This is the actual track where you raced, right, Mom?"

"That's it, yes. Of course it looked much different when I raced here. The infield was a large green meadow, practically empty. With small paddocks for the racehorses and a covered pavilion for the owners and jockeys for protection from the rain and the sun. It was a place for picnics, kids to play. I think it looked more beautiful then. Yes, I spent much of my youth right here. I did high school homework in that meadow."

Kim gazed across the infield. "Remember the day, Bao, when father led those little ones around on the horses?" she said.

"Yes, I do." He smiled at the thought, then turned more serious and said, "But it was the war then, Kim. The days were not so happy. That's about the time we lost Mi."

"Yes, Mi was a fine boy. Always a good friend to our family. I know he meant a lot to you."

"Mom, the track is huge!"

"It's huge and your mom was a star here," Charlie added. They passed the track area, continued on Plantation Road and soon turned off, heading to the original Sun Stone Horse Farm where Bao and Tam and their family still lived.

When they reached the farm, Kim remarked that little had changed in twenty years except more land was cultivated in vegetables and rice, instead of pasture land and horse hay. Tam and Lia came out to greet them. Introductions were made and the luggage carried in. They freshened up and retired to the sitting room for drinks, except for Kim and Bao. Kim wanted to stroll a little around the farm with her brother.

Kim said, "I'm so glad you were able to save the farm, Bao. I'm sure father was very proud you did that."

"Yes, that was good. But we have Tam to thank for that also. I wouldn't have been able to keep the farm without her. We were married just before the final hectic months of the old government."

"How did all that happen with you and Tam, Bao?"

"Things became very crazy at the end of 1974 and into 1975," Bao said. "It seemed everyone in Saigon was trying to get out. Mother and Father had decided they would stay. It was their home, Vietnam was in their blood. They had picked up and moved to a new life twenty years before. They agreed they were too old to do that again. They were hoping they were old enough for the new government to ignore. Or if not, they would be shown mercy. If they died in their house, so be it.

"About that time, Tam's mother died. She had cancer and suffered greatly, as I understand it. I hadn't seen Tam for more than two years, since the day on the street in 1972 before you left. She had no money, the Viet Minh had abandoned her, her kids were on the point of starving."

"So those little ones were Tam's?"

"Yes, I think most people knew that, anyway. I'm sure Charlie thought that. By the way those two 'little ones' are now both at City University downtown."

"Well done, Bao."

"Thanks. To go on, Tam contacted me, and laid it all out: had two kids that she would never leave, no money, said she was done with the Viet Minh and wanted a new life. I helped her with a little money. We started seeing each other and decided to get married. I would only tell this to you, Kim, but it was something I'd dreamed of since the first day I saw her at the University. I honestly think she did, too. You know she's very Catholic. Now you can see us at Mass in the basilica every Sunday morning. Never thought you'd see that!"

Bao said, "It's worked out fine. Mother and Father always loved her kids, and Tam was a great help when the government changed in 1975. When the new regime took over and started checking into who owned what and who did what during the war, Tam had some great Viet Minh contacts that supported us."

"It's a wonderful story, Bao. I'm glad it all worked out. Whatever happened to Black Martin?"

"In 1975, when the new regime came in, the horse racing was stopped by order of the government. Father sold all the horses except for Black Martin. The others were sold as cart horses. Black Martin was allowed to be kept, ostensibly for farm use. Actually, he was a pet for father, who hoped that horse racing would return. The horse was a fine part of the family, especially for the kids. He died perhaps five years ago. A sad day for the family. He'd kept the memories alive."

"Yes, he was a good horse. I remember him as though it were yesterday. Thanks for that, Bao, I'm afraid it made me a little emotional," she said as she dabbed her eyes. "Shall we join the others?"

Kim wanted to see Tam. She joined her in the kitchen with her daughter Lia. "Where do you go to school, Lia?"

"Saint Augustine, in the city."

"No! It's my old school!"

"Yes; my father told me; he went there, too."

"Yes, and he got better grades than I. Is Sister Anna Marie still there?"

"I don't think so, I've never heard of her."

Kim said, "Well, she would be pretty old by now."

Lia left the room to do her homework.

"It's a shame we didn't get to know each other back then, Tam," Kim said.

"Yes, it is, but my life was a mess then. I was such a wild kid it's probably better we didn't. I was a real rebel. I took up with a boy after my father was killed in the war. We were so young and wild, we married on the spur of the moment. It wasn't a real marriage. He was gone most of the time; two kids came fast. The boy left for good and my mom helped me care for them, until she got sick. We had nothing, we all walked from Cau Mau deep in the south to Saigon to escape the war. We searched the whole way to Saigon for food and shelter. It was horrible. I made some terrible mistakes and choices. Someone must have been watching out for me."

"Yes, but you were a good mother to your children. It all turned out for the best. It's a gift that you and Bao found each other and I owe you a debt of gratitude for helping my parents all these years."

A funeral Mass of Christian burial took place the following morning in the familiar basilica, downtown. Binh's family had been

Chapter Three

active members of that parish since the 1950s. Their parish priest, well known to all family members, presided. There were more attendees than expected. Many families from the parish who had known Binh over the years, as well as a few friends of Kim and Bao, were there. Some of the old-timers from the former Saigon Racing Association attended.

Charlie felt comfortable in the beautiful basilica with its pristine white marble, the feeling of deep reverence and the good memories of years ago. They occupied the front pew, near the magnificent alter.

On the way out, Charlie's family of three diverted to the north wall in the rear of the church. Charlie wanted to show Therese the statue of Saint Michael that he had admired and below where he'd prayed for guidance during the war. As he and Kim passed the rear alcove, she and Charlie smiled at their secret memory. Charlie was pleased the statue had been recently cleaned and looked magnificent. He explained to Therese the multitude of plaques on the North wall, which exclaimed 'Merci,' below the likeness of Saint Michael.

"It means, 'Thanks be to the Lord' for perhaps a precious gift received, a prayer answered, or perhaps an injustice corrected by an anonymous donor. It could be for just about anything."

Therese asked, "Could it be for a life well lived, for Grandfather Binh? I am truly amazed at the things I've heard about him in the last two days."

"Of course it could, Therese. A wonderful thought."

They returned to the farm for a small gathering of many of the friends and others who knew Binh and wanted to express kind thoughts of him or a remembrance of a kindness. Charlie and Kim were emotionally and physically drained when most of the crowd had left. Along with Therese, they collapsed on the settee in the front room.

Bao walked in and joined them. He took Binh's favorite chair across from the settee. Kim said, "You are now the patriarch of the family, Bao. You look good in Father's chair."

"No, I'll never think of this chair as anything but Father's." Pause, then, "Incidentally, from this chair I see the box of mementos that Father wanted your family to have, Kim. Remind me to put that in the jeep when we return to the airport."

Charlie looked over at the cardboard box, and said, "Well, let's take a look." He opened the box and saw one of the old racing saddles Kim had used. He pulled it out so Therese could examine it. It was quite light in weight and he handed it to her. Below the saddle were Binh's old Foreign Legion boots.

Bao explained, "Father said maybe someone in your family could use those on your farm."

Charlie pulled out one of the boots and examined it.

"I remember Father would allow those soles to be replaced only at Duc Long's, on Le Thanh Ton Street," Kim said. "It's where he bought your briefcase, Charlie."

"They've been resoled many times."

Charlie looked inside the boot and saw a label that read, *NOIR-JEAN and MONTADE, Military Footwear, Normandie, France*. Then Charlie saw another label, just below the manufacturer's label, that looked like a nametag. It was worn and more difficult to read.

He brushed off the dust and read it as:

Xavier Martin Duvall
Foreign Legion Forces
Republic of France

Chapter Three

Charlie studied the name for a few seconds, then became quiet. He felt a chill run through his body as he began to absorb the first taste of an unexpected and shocking truth. He read the name out loud, "Xavier Martin Duvall. That's my father's name," he said calmly. The room became quiet. Turning to Bao, he asked, "What did your father call his French friend?"

"The Frenchman."

"When did the Frenchman return to France?"

"It was after the Japanese left Vietnam," Bao replied. "In 1946."

"My parents were married in France in 1947. I was born in 1947. My father was killed soon after. These boots belonged to my real father."

The room was quiet for a few seconds, as the discovery sank in. Then Charlie said, "The Frenchman was my father."

He looked at Kim who was staring at him and said, "You know what this means, Kim … "

"Yes … your father and mine were friends, and soldiers together, in Vietnam."

Charlie and Kim were up early next morning. Their return flight to the States departed at 12:30 p.m. It was a beautiful sunrise and a crisp morning, a great day for flying. A brief walk down the lane to the provincial road would be a pleasure before the hustle and bustle of the day began. They left the house when all were still sleeping and began their stroll. A pleasant coolness surrounded them as they walked. Morning dew was radiant on the wildflower pedals as the new sun caught them at a low angle, warmed them, and in minutes they moved on. They passed a couple of large trees that had developed high branches in the last two decades that now covered the lane high above.

Kim said, "I love this place. I guess it's true that one doesn't realize how much one has until it's gone."

"Would you like to live here, Kim? Make our home here someday, in Vietnam?"

"Well, I wouldn't rule it out. But maybe live here half a year and Ithaca the other half."

Charlie said honestly, "I could live with that."

They reached the road and turned around. They walked slowly in silence enjoying the walk for the next few minutes.

Kim said, "Charlie ... do you remember when we were hiding in that barn and whispering to keep our courage up, and I asked you why you came to Vietnam?"

"I do."

"Do you remember what you told me?"

"I think I told you I came for a lot of reasons."

"Yes, and you said one of those reasons was to honor your birth father who fought in WWII. I was thinking last night after we talked about him. I remember I told you in that barn I felt my life changed when I first met you. I felt a kind of destiny in you. It was strange, I felt I was now safely on a wonderful trajectory that was going to be my life. And I was comfortable with that."

"It's strange what life presents us with sometimes. When I landed here years ago, for some reason I felt it was the beginning of a great adventure. I don't know why. But I felt something big was going to happen to me here. I felt this was the place in time where I was supposed to be."

"Do you believe in miracles, Charlie?"

Chapter Three

"Miracles? I believe there is a reason for everything. But sometimes things that happen seem to have no explanation. They seem to be great mysteries. Are they miracles, or are they things that were just meant to be? Because of a number of things in my life, I decided to join the Navy. If I hadn't, I would never have met you. And after last night, I've begun to think I was drawn to Vietnam because our fathers were friends here. It's hard to explain this."

Kim said, "Like you, I have this feeling that all of us coming together here: you and I, my father, and your father was meant to be."

She looked up at him and said in a genuine way, "Would that be … a miracle?"

He turned and said, "Yes. How else could we explain it?"

Epilogue

The fictional tale of Charlie and Kim ends in this book but, of course, the story of Vietnam continued. The Paris Peace Accords was eventually signed in January, 1973. Most believed the agreement wouldn't hold. It didn't. The Americans went home. The American POWs came home. But fighting resumed immediately and two years later—in April of 1975—North Vietnam together with the Viet Minh overran South Vietnam.

The country was unified as one communist state called the Socialist Republic of Vietnam (SRV) under the Communist Party of Vietnam (CPV). North Vietnam prevailed, but there were no winners in the Vietnam War. The country was left with a staggering death toll of millions (civilians and military) and a land devastated by massive bombing. Many in the south fled, fearing the worst, and became for years migrants without a country. And as we know, there were 58,000

Americans killed and hundreds of thousands physically and/or mentally wounded.

The bloodbath expected in South Vietnam did not materialize, but the new regime punished military officers and political dissidents from the former system by sending them to "re-education" camps for up to fifteen years. The camps were a heavy dose of party indoctrination, hard labor, and harsh living. Unfortunately, many young bright and educated Vietnamese officers such as Dao and Danh would have been sent to these camps while their families struggled on alone. The government eradicated private trade and commerce and nationalized private industry and infrastructure. The CPV clamped down on religion and entertainment. A communist collective system of agriculture seized privately owned farms. Rural people like the characters of Binh and Therese and their rural friends would have been forced to give up most of their land, farming equipment, and livestock to collective government planners.

The war-torn country, with a worsening economy, struggled on in a dark period for the next ten years. Food shortages and poverty increased. The people resisted the communist approach of collectivization of agriculture and government ownership of the small industries and gradually a more market-driven economy began to creep in. Things improved slowly. By the 1980s, private farms and agriculture and small industries began to re-emerge. International travel in and out of Vietnam began to open up in the early 1980s, and by 1986 the government eased visa restrictions for international travel. Also in 1986, the CPV officially relaxed its economic grip and introduced a program called "Doi Moi," a system of political and economic changes that moved away from central control to a market-driven approach. A model more like that of China.

Epilogue

By 1991, travel would not have been a problem for Charlie and Kim in their trip to Vietnam to attend her father's funeral. In 1994, the US government eliminated the trade embargo leveled after the war and in 1995 re-established official diplomatic relations with the new government of Vietnam.

Time has moved on, and with it Vietnam has one of the fastest growing economies in the world. Most of the old leaders of the communist regime have retired or passed away. A new generation with new ideas and techniques in economics have replaced the old. Today, Vietnam has a market-driven economy and large, solid economic sectors which export agriculture, hi-tech manufacturing, and garment industry products. Its natural resources of white beaches, blue waters, and mountainous geography in a tropical setting have made it a prime tourist destination.

And so it's been nearly fifty years since the time of the story of Charlie and his sweetheart Kim, the young girl from the racetrack. Most of the population of Vietnam now has little or no memory of the Vietnam War. They are too young. They are, like me, trying to remember World War II. It's always been ancient history. We learn of these things in books or from documentaries on PBS or some elderly grandfather or great uncle who may have even been present in the terrifying reality of those moments during the war we later read about.

In Vietnam I feel reasonably sure that at this moment there is an elderly grandfather that has been helped to a quiet glade in the old Saigon Zoo and botanical gardens and is sitting quietly on a concrete bench, cane at his side, enjoying a pool of exotic fish. He remembers these things and those he fought with and relied on and the hopes they had for their country.

These old grandfathers and great-uncles with white hair and beautiful old faces of tan wrinkled skin pulled tightly over cheek bones were once young and vibrant and filled with enthusiasm. They had dreams and aspirations of interesting careers in politics, engineering, agriculture, art and literature. They believed in America and the country called the Republic of Vietnam—a country that no longer exists.

But they also must sit and think and ponder the meaning of it all, and perhaps they take some solace in remembering that they did what they were supposed to do in their lives and feel some vindication as they look at the progressive country that is now Vietnam, realizing they had a part in testing the limits of political and economic systems in societies. They produced the new generation that resisted the communist theories of social reforms and developed the modern economic systems that brought advances in agriculture and built the gleaming skyscrapers and the high-tech manufacturing centers.

They must think the irony astounding.